"What kind of comfort are you offering me, Wynne?"

She glanced up into his eyes. The cold, calculated hardness in them—so at odds with his touch and his words—made her shrink back inside of herself. She took a step away from him, tugging her hand free. "Not that kind of comfort."

Her voice sounded like it belonged to somebody else.

"Are you sure?"

How could he make his voice so warm when his eyes were so hard?

"Positive."

"Because I do not fraternize with my staff."

She prickled at the threat latent in his words—that if she attempted to *fraternize* with him, he'd see it as grounds for instant dismissal. She couldn't be dismissed. Not yet.

She drew herself up to her full height. "If by *fraternize* you mean *sleep with*, then let me assure you that you're safe from me." She whirled around and made for the conference room. "You're not my type," she hurled over her shoulder.

Dear Reader,

I've always been intrigued by the idea of a prior generation's actions coming back to haunt the current generation, which is what happens to Wynne and Xavier in *The Spanish Tycoon's Takeover*. Wynne's grandmother and Xavier's grandfather have had "dealings" with each other in the past—fifty years ago to be precise—and the fallout from that time leaves our trusty heroine and hero feeling that the ground beneath their feet is less than solid.

However, one of the things I so love about the romance genre is that themes of forgiveness abound. Within the pages of a romance novel, we can discover understanding and empathy... and love. Before Wynne and Xavier can win love, however, they need to decide whether they'll follow in the footsteps of their much-loved elders...or whether they have the courage to forge a new path that leads to each other.

This is a story about two strong people who have very different but equally worthwhile goals. Love is a risk...but it's a risk worth taking when you find the right person. And for Wynne and Xavier, love sneaks up on them when they're least expecting it.

I have my fingers crossed that you will love Wynne and Xavier's story as much as I do.

Hugs,

Michelle

The Spanish Tycoon's Takeover

—

Michelle Douglas

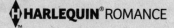

Recycling programs
for this product may
not exist in your area.

ISBN-13: 978-0-373-74430-5

The Spanish Tycoon's Takeover

First North American Publication 2017

Copyright © 2017 by Michelle Douglas

Printed in U.S.A.

www.Harlequin.com

Michelle Douglas has been writing for Harlequin since 2007 and believes she has the best job in the world. She lives in a leafy suburb of Newcastle, on Australia's east coast, with her own romantic hero, a house full of dust and books, and an eclectic collection of '60s and '70s vinyl. She loves to hear from readers and can be contacted via her website, michelle-douglas.com.

Books by Michelle Douglas

Harlequin Romance

The Vineyards of Calanetti
Reunited by a Baby Secret

The Wild Ones
Her Irresistible Protector
The Rebel and the Heiress

Bellaroo Creek!
The Cattleman's Ready-Made Family

Mothers in a Million
First Comes Baby...

The Man Who Saw Her Beauty
Bella's Impossible Boss
The Nanny Who Saved Christmas
The Redemption of Rico D'Angelo
Road Trip with the Eligible Bachelor
Snowbound Surprise for the Billionaire
The Millionaire and the Maid
A Deal to Mend Their Marriage
An Unlikely Bride for the Billionaire

Visit the Author Profile page
at Harlequin.com for more titles.

To Janet, who always champions the underdog and expects no thanks in return. You're an inspiration.

CHAPTER ONE

WYNNE STEPHENS TURNED a full circle on the spot, pressing a hand to her churning stomach. The foyer of Aggie's Retreat gleamed. She should be proud.

But, even looking at it through her usual rose-tinted glasses, she knew the sparkling cleanliness couldn't hide the fact that the carpet on the stairs leading to the first-floor rooms was badly worn and starting to fray, or that the ornate double doors leading into what a brass plaque grandly pronounced as *The Drawing Room* were such poor Victorian imitations as to be almost laughable. The pounding at her temples increased.

To make matters worse, the skylight above them flooded the foyer with so much Queensland Gold Coast sunshine as to completely counter the motel's cosy Victorian manor theme.

No, no—sunlight is good.

Sunlight was a mood-enhancer, right? She wanted Xavier Mateo Ramos in as good a mood as possible. And why shouldn't he be? He'd just bought her pride and joy.

'I thought he'd be here by now.' Tina drummed her fingers repeatedly against the back of the stool she stood behind.

Wynne couldn't sit either. She moved behind the

check-in counter to tidy the tourist brochures arranged on a discreet stand at its far end. They didn't
need tidying, but her hands needed to be busy. She
tried to keep her face smooth, despite the pounding at her temples and the nausea swirling in her
stomach.

She managed a shrug. Whether she managed
nonchalance, though, was debatable.

'He didn't give an exact time for his arrival.'
She'd been expecting a text for the last couple of
hours, but though she'd kept checking one hadn't
arrived. She checked her phone again all the same.

'It's a long flight from Spain. Maybe he and his
party decided to stay over in Sydney for another
day.'

'I wish he'd stay there forever!'

Wynne tried to send her front-of-house reception clerk and right-hand woman a buck-up smile,
but if the narrowing of Tina's eyes was anything
to go by she hadn't succeeded.

'I have a bad feeling about this.' Tina thumped
down to the stool. 'If your grandmother knew she'd
have kittens, and—'

'But my grandmother *doesn't* know,' Wynne cut
in, her heart twisting. 'She's never going to know.
She…'

Her voice cracked and she coughed to cover it.
She pressed her lips together, afraid that if she said
another word the burning at the backs of her eyes
would get the better of her. If Aggie knew Wynne

had sold her beloved motel she'd… Well, there was no knowing what she'd do. Aggie had always been unpredictable in everything except her love for Aggie's Retreat and for Wynne. One thing was certain, though—it would break her heart.

Wynne pulled in a deep breath. Alzheimer's disease, however, ensured that Aggie would *never* know.

'I'm sorry.' Tina reached across to squeeze her hand. 'That wasn't fair of me.'

She knew what Tina was really thinking, but was too tactful to voice—*Would it really have been so bad to move Aggie from her expensive private nursing home to a cheaper facility?* If she'd done so, she wouldn't have had to sell Aggie's Retreat.

Wynne hoped that she lived a further thirty-three years before she was called upon to make another such soul-destroying decision—a damned if she did and damned if she didn't decision: to keep the motel that was her beloved grandmother's legacy or to ensure that her grandmother's comfort and what little happiness remained to her was secured.

God forgive her, but she'd chosen the latter.

And today she'd come face to face with the man who'd bought Aggie's Retreat.

Darkness threatened the edges of her vision and she had to concentrate on her breathing in an effort to counter it. *You will not faint!*

It wasn't even that she cared so much for herself, but the sale of the motel didn't only affect *her*, and that knowledge tormented her. She could start over easily enough. She was relatively young. She had plenty of experience in the industry. As hard as it would be to walk away from Aggie's Retreat, she'd find another position in the blink of an eye if she needed to. But her staff…

Dear God! She pressed both hands to her stomach. She'd been told by more than one person in the industry that she employed *the dregs of society*. Her nostrils flared. She knew *exactly* what it was like to be considered *not good enough*. Her mother mightn't have said the words out loud, but her actions had sent a loud and clear message. Duncan hadn't had any such qualms. He hadn't minced his words when he'd told her she wasn't polished enough, sophisticated enough, *good enough* to mix in his world.

She swallowed. Her staff had proved over and over again that they were more than capable of doing the jobs assigned to them. She owed them. And she was determined that they would all rise above the spiteful criticisms and petty insults and prove exactly how worthy they were.

She just needed to convince her new boss to give them a chance. That was all.

She glanced across at Tina. 'I know you're worried about your position here, but I'm sure it's as safe as houses.'

She said it with more confidence than she felt, but Xavier Ramos *had* signed her to a two-year contract as the motel's manager. Which surely gave her hiring and firing rights. In which case Tina wouldn't be going anywhere. Nor would April or Libby or Meg or Justin or Graeme.

Wynne crossed her fingers and her toes. Tina needed this job. She was locked in a vicious custody battle with her despicable ex-husband. This job not only provided proof of Tina's ability to provide financially for herself and her children, but the flexibility in her hours meant she had few childcare worries.

'What if he decides to bring in his own people?'

'Like who? He's Spanish. He doesn't have *his own people*. At least not here in Australia. *We're* his people.'

But they both knew that with a single snap of his fingers he could toss them all out on their ears. Their new boss had the wherewithal to throw around more money in a day than either she or Tina would make in ten years combined. Men like that set their own rules.

Wynne straightened. He *had* agreed to hire her as manager, and that would give her the opportunity to fight for the staff, to make a case for them if need be, to make him listen.

Tina scowled. 'These tycoon types *always* have their own people. He probably comes from one of those huge extended families. I bet he has an army of nephews and nieces, aunts and uncles and endless cousins who all need jobs. There…there might even be an arm of the family that's scandalous… and he's looking for a way to exile them overseas… and means to use Aggie's Retreat as a bribe. There could be vendettas and—'

Wynne started to laugh. 'You've been watching too many soap operas. I hope he gets here soon, because we're both starting to play the worst-case scenario game.'

Tina thrust her jaw out. 'What if he decides to turn Aggie's Retreat into one of those signature Ramos extravagances? None of us will come up to scratch if that happens.'

Unfortunately that was true. But… 'This place is too small.'

If the Ramos chain had decided to move into the Gold Coast market with one of their signature hotels, they wouldn't have chosen a tiny little motor inn as their starting point.

'Aggie's Retreat—' she glanced around wondering why Xavier had bought it without even seeing it '—is way too small scale for the Ramos chain.'

'I wish you'd been able to find out more,' Tina grumbled.

So did Wynne. While she'd shared an extensive email and phone correspondence with Xavier, he'd been tight-lipped about his plans for the motel. She pulled in a breath.

'Things will change—that's inevitable—but some of those changes will be for the better. At least all the endless repairs that have started piling up will get done.' And not before time. No longer to worry about leaky taps, wonky wiring and broken roof tiles—what bliss!

She sent Tina a suddenly mischievous grin. 'Who knows? He might even make over the motel in a Spanish style.'

Tina finally laughed. 'Aggie's dream! Now, that *would* be fun.'

Wynne rubbed damp palms down the sides of her black trousers. 'And don't forget he assured me that our vision for the motel was in line. Why on earth would he hire me on a two-year contract otherwise?'

'To get you to sign on the dotted line.'

But *why*? Why would someone with the Ramos name want this little old motor inn of no account?

She hadn't questioned it too much at the time, had simply been grateful that the sale would provide her with the financial wherewithal to take care of her grandmother. She squared her shoulders.

'Let's stop second-guessing the man. Our questions will get answered soon enough. Today we're simply going to wow him with our renowned hospitality.'

Tina gave a nod, before sending Wynne a sidelong glance. 'Aren't you even a little bit nervous about meeting him?'

She wanted to deny it, but found herself running a hand across her chest in a useless effort to ease the tension that had it clenched up tight.

'Terrified.' She clenched and unclenched her hands. 'I thought signing the sale contract would be the worst moment in this whole sorry business, but this is coming in a very close second.'

Tina hugged her. 'I'm sorry. I've been a tact-less cow.'

'Nonsense. You're as nervous as I am—that's all. And just as invested.'

But the moment Xavier Ramos strode through the front door Wynne would no longer be the owner of Aggie's Retreat. Technically she wasn't the owner now, but it wouldn't feel real until Xavier strode through those doors to stake claim to it.

A black pit opened up inside her.

'Misses! Miss Wynne! Miss Tina!' Libby came clattering down the stairs from the first floor.

'No running!' Wynne and Tina shouted at the same time.

'Sorry, Miss Wynne. Sorry, Miss Tina.' Their exhortations barely dimmed Libby's Labrador-puppy-like excitement. 'Miss April told me to tell you a limer…limo…that a big fancy car is coming down the street.'

Wynne's heart started to hammer and she envied Libby her big, guileless smile. Libby was one of the team of young Down Syndrome workers that Wynne had hired from a local shelter. They formed a significant part of the housekeeping and gardening staff. April, her housekeeping manager, had been hired on a prison release parole programme.

As had her maintenance man Justin. Tina and Meg had been hired from an agency that placed women who were victims of domestic abuse into the workforce. The dregs of society? Not likely!

She swallowed. They were her family. She loved them.

And yet she'd put her grandmother first. That knowledge—the guilt—ate away at her. She had to do her best for them. Better than her best.

She would *not* let her new boss fire them.

'Thank you, Libby. Now, back upstairs with you and thank April for the warning. And no running this time.'

With a grin, Libby set off upstairs again, though thankfully at a more sedate pace.

How will you stop him? If he wants to fire them, how will you stop him?

She'd think of something. But hopefully it wouldn't be necessary.

Through the expanse of glass at the front of the building she and Tina watched a long white limousine move down the drive, past the row of Christmas palms, to slide to a smooth halt by the front doors.

'Good luck to us,' Tina whispered. 'I'm saying prayers…lots of prayers.'

Wynne moved out from behind the reception desk—a long curved confection of pine masquerading as polished oak—and then wasn't sure what she should do. Hovering in the foyer like this made her feel like a fool.

She glanced around the faux Victorian interior and, as always, it made her smile. The Axminster carpet might be faded, and there might be the odd crack in the plasterwork, but the wooden staircase gleamed with the same rich lustre as the reception desk, the ginormous vase of gladioli looked stately on its marble stand, while the ornate mirror above them reflected an abundance of light over the space. The one thing Aggie's Retreat did well was its welcome.

Wynne turned as a tall figure encased in an impeccable business suit strode through the door held open for him by his chauffeur. He stopped and surveyed the foyer through narrowed eyes, his chin held at an arrogant angle. His nostrils flared and light briefly blazed in his eyes before it was abruptly checked.

Wynne blinked—and swallowed. Dear Lord, the man was tall. And…um…broad. Dark eyes speared her with a steely gaze. Very slowly he moved towards her, and the closer he came the more he reminded her of something primal and immovable—like a mountain. Such a large man had no right to move with such panther-like grace. She flashed to a vision of him bursting the seams at the shoulders and arms of his jacket like the Incredible Hulk. Except…

Except he looked far too controlled and forbidding to do anything so unpremeditated.

Resisting the urge to run a finger around the collar of her blouse, she forced herself forward and made her smile broad. After all this was the new owner of Aggie's Retreat. He deserved a welcome fit for royalty.

'You must be Mr Ramos.'

He took her outstretched hand without hesitation, and this close to him she felt her pulse kick and her heart crash. He was the most disconcerting combination of hot and cold she'd ever come across. Despite the forbidding remoteness in his eyes, he had the whole simmering Mediterranean smoky sex appeal thing down pat.

'Call me Xavier.'

The words fired out of him, clipped and curt—an order rather than a request. Her spine stiffened, until she reminded herself that he'd only flown in from Spain two days ago. Jet lag probably had him desperately discombobulated. And he *was* her boss. He could issue orders with gay abandon and she would simply have to bite her tongue and pretend that she wanted nothing more than to do his bidding.

She willed her body to relax. *For the staff's sake.*

'I'm Wynne Stephens. It's lovely to finally meet you in person.'

He inclined his head and his hair gleamed as dark as the sea at midnight—jet-black. She'd never seen hair so dark. It looked thick and soft, and the tips of her fingers started to tingle.

His eyes were just as dark as his hair. The heat

from his hand burned against her palm. But despite their darkness and depth his eyes remained cool. His lips had barely moved upwards into a smile, and she must have been watching too many B-grade movies recently, because she could swear she imagined a hint of cruelty about his mouth.

Those dark eyes scanned her face and she felt as if every secret she'd ever had was being pulled out for his examination and judgement. Heat travelled up her arm and she realised her hand was still clasped in his. She tugged it free, working overtime to hold fast to her composure.

'You have a very attractive…'

Movement in the doorway captured her attention—the chauffeur, struggling in with a variety of luggage. Should she go and help him?

'Ms Stephens?'

'Oh!' She swung back to him. 'You must call me Wynne.'

His lips thinned. 'I have a very attractive…?'

She choked back a laugh. Nothing like leaving a sentence hanging! 'Accent.' It was even better in person than on the phone.

One eyebrow lifted with devastating irony. 'Really?'

She stared up at him and the derision in his eyes made heat rush into her face. Oh, he couldn't think that she…

No way! He was attractive, but…

Suddenly the images flashing through Wynne's mind became just a little too vivid.

She shook her head to dispel them, to try and get back on track. 'Xavier, I'd like to welcome you to Aggie's Retreat.'

He didn't answer, just continued to stare at her with those pitiless eyes.

She lifted her chin, pushed her shoulders back. 'I sincerely hope the motel brings you as much joy and pleasure as it has over the years to my grandmother and myself.'

Those lips cracked open into a ruthless smile that had her suppressing a shiver.

'Don't worry, Wynne, it already has.'

Wynne glanced past him and some of the tension in Xavier's jaw eased. The wholeheartedness of her smile, its warmth, had taken him completely off-guard. He'd not expected her to be so…generous.

She'd not wanted to sell the motel—her reluctance had threaded through their every email and telephone exchange. It was no doubt why she'd made being manager one of the stipulations of the sale. His fists clenched. That still angered him, but it could be dealt with easily enough over the coming weeks. And it would be.

He'd arrived here today expecting tears…had readied himself for hostility. Instead…

He fought back a frown. Instead he'd been welcomed with a warmth that had made him want to turn around and return to Spain. She made him feel… He swallowed. For a moment she'd made him feel the same way his grandfather had always made him feel—truly welcome.

A dark weariness threatened to descend over him—an all too familiar grief that he'd wrestled with for the past four weeks and two days. It would be weak to give in to it, but it rose up within him now with renewed force as he glanced into Wynne Stephens's face. He wanted to accept the welcome she offered. He wanted to embrace it and hold it tight.

It was a lie, though. She didn't *know* him. She didn't *care* for him. But that didn't make the need gaping through him go away.

Dios! His hand clenched into a fist. He'd readied himself for a fight—a dirty fight—and she'd pulled the carpet out from under him. She'd welcomed him to Aggie's Retreat as if she'd meant it. The woman was a witch! Just like her grandmother.

He stiffened, forcing up a wall between himself and his new manager. He always built a wall between himself and bewitching women. It kept things simple.

With a Herculean effort he kept the frown from his face, refusing to reveal his surprise, refusing to reveal how she'd thrown him. He'd seen her photograph. He'd known that she was attractive. But attractive women were everywhere. In his world *beautiful* women were everywhere. What Wynne Stephens's photograph *hadn't* revealed was the life and animation that filled the woman, threaded through her with a vibrancy that made what she looked like a secondary consideration. He hadn't expected that.

If she wasn't a Stephens…

He pushed the thought aside. He had no intention of punishing Wynne for her grandmother's crimes, but a part of him couldn't resist glorying in the knowledge that the world had come full circle—that a Ramos now had a Stephens under his thumb.

He hoped his grandfather was looking down and laughing with the pleasure of it. He hoped it would allow his grandfather finally to find peace.

Don't make the same mistakes I made.

I won't, he swore silently.

He realised the silence in the foyer had grown too long and uncomfortable. Not that he cared too much about that. It suited him to make others uncomfortable. It made them pause for thought before lying or double-crossing him.

He gestured behind him. 'This is Reyes, my driver.'

Wynne welcomed him to Australia too, her words accompanied with one of those big smiles. Xavier made sure to survey it only from the corner of his eyes. He had to meet her gaze head-on, though, when she turned it back to him.

'I thought from your correspondence that your son and his nanny would be accompanying you too.'

'They will be arriving later.'

She stared at him as if waiting for more. 'Later… today?'

'No.'

She stared some more, as if waiting for him to continue, but he refused to gratify her curiosity. He'd left Luis in Sydney, under the eagle eye of his nanny Paula. He'd given them free rein to sightsee for the next few days. He hadn't wanted to bring Luis here to witness any potential unpleasantness. And, while the welcome hadn't been unpleasant, he had no doubt that the next few days would be.

'Right. Well…make sure to let us know when to expect them.'

'Why?'

She blinked. 'So that we can have their room ready, of course.'

One of those megawatt smiles slammed into him.

'And so we can make a fuss.'

Her laugh! It could wrap around a man and make him want— *Nonsense!*

'No fuss will be necessary.'

Her smile only widened. 'That's what *you* think.' Her blonde hair bounced about her shoulders and down her back, crackling with life and energy, as she gestured to the woman behind the counter.

'This is Tina, and we're both determined to make your stay here as enjoyable as we can.'

He nodded at the other woman.

'Now, tell me what you would most like? We've organised afternoon tea in the Drawing Room if you'd like refreshments. Tea, coffee, lamingtons—which are an Australian speciality—and chocolate chip cookies because...' She shrugged. 'We were expecting Luis, and what little boy can resist those, right?'

Xavier stared at the woman, dumbfounded. He'd just bought her motel. He wasn't dropping in for *tea*!

She must have misread his expression, because he received another blast of warmth from that spectacular smile of hers. 'We knew you'd probably be exhausted, and thought you might want a little pick-me-up before you took a tour of the place.'

'We would prefer it if you simply showed us to our rooms.'

Her smile slipped, but only for a second. For that second, though, he felt like the worst of heels.

'Of course.'

'You can send refreshments to our rooms.'

A wall came down in her eyes then, though nothing else in her expression changed, and he bit back something rude. He'd meant his words to come out as sign of appreciation for the refreshments she'd organised, not as a command.

He glanced around, resisting the urge to roll his shoulders. 'Where is your bellboy or a porter?'

Her laugh feathered across his skin. 'Ah, that would be me.'

Before he could say anything she took one of the suitcases that Reyes had placed on the floor and started up the stairs.

'Your rooms are right this way. I've made sure you have the very best rooms Aggie's Retreat has to offer.' A twinkle lit her eyes as she glanced back over her shoulder to Xavier. 'I fear, however, that it'll be a little more rustic than you're used to.'

In two strides he was at her side and had relieved her of the suitcase. It was all he could do not to scowl at her. 'You think I will find fault with my quarters?'

'Absolutely not.' There was a hint of mischief in her eyes. 'I expect the motel to charm your socks off!'

A quaint expression, perhaps, but her optimism was misplaced. He kept silent on that point, however.

She led them to the very end of the first floor corridor, and he refused to notice the provocative sway of her hips. Had she deliberately placed them in the rooms furthest from reception?

She flung open a door to her right. 'This is the Windsor Suite. Our best room, and yours for the duration, Xavier.'

He'd seen pictures of all the rooms, of course.

But this wasn't a suite. There were no separate bedroom and living quarters. The sleeping area was merely separated from the living area by a step, and the most ludicrous wooden railing that stretched from one side of the room to the other. A sliding glass door gave on to a balcony overlooking the rear of the motel. It was decorated with what he suspected were fake wrought-iron railings and fretwork. Still, it would do for now.

'Opposite we have Luis and Paula's room—the Westminster Suite—for when they arrive.'

She opened the door for his inspection. It was large, like his, and contained two double beds. Rather than a balcony it had a sunroom that overlooked the front of the motel. Reyes's room—the Cambridge Suite—was next to it.

'I hope you'll be very comfortable. I'll send up refreshments shortly. If there's anything you need, just ring down to Reception.'

'Thank you.' He nodded. 'Today we will settle in. Tomorrow we will get to work.'

By the time he was through there wouldn't be a trace of the black-hearted Aggie Stephens left in this godforsaken motor inn. He couldn't wait to get started. He would turn Aggie's Retreat into a haven of such beauty and opulence that his grandfather's name would be linked with innovation and luxury forever.

He would do his grandfather's memory proud. He would turn this into a place that Lorenzo would have loved—an establishment worthy of him. Once that was done maybe the scalding ache that had taken up residence in his chest since Lorenzo's death would finally go away.

CHAPTER TWO

XAVIER SET A deliberately ruthless pace the following morning. He wanted to gauge Wynne's measure before he set about incorporating the changes that would turn this two-bit motor inn into one of the most extravagantly luxurious hotels in the Ramos Corporation's portfolio.

His grandfather deserved the best.

In his final days Lorenzo had confided in Xavier—had confessed that for the past fifty-five years this was where his heart had dwelled. He'd smiled at Xavier with such sadness it had been all Xavier could do not to throw his head back and howl.

Don't make the same mistakes I made.

He'd made his grandson promise. Xavier had pressed his hand to his heart and had sworn he wouldn't. That promise had brought his grandfather a measure of peace. For himself, Xavier had sworn to find a way to pay fitting tribute to the only person who had truly loved him.

No expense would be spared.

Nor would recalcitrant employees.

Xavier had ordered Wynne to dance attendance on him at eight a.m., but she'd cheerfully informed him that that was impossible—she had breakfasts to take care of. The earliest she'd be free would be nine o'clock, once Tina's shift started.

To her credit, she'd arrived in the motel's conference room—located next to his suite—at nine on the dot. As he'd demanded his own breakfast at six-thirty he knew she must have been up for at least three and a half hours, but she'd tripped in as fresh and perky as if she'd only just started her day. He wasn't quite sure why, but it had annoyed him.

'Tell me the deal with your breakfasts,' he ordered now, without preamble.

She gestured to a chair. 'May I sit?' Her eyes danced. 'Or am I to stand in front of the headmaster as I'm grilled to within an inch of my life?'

He blinked.

She didn't wait for his invitation, but took the seat opposite. She crossed her legs and folded her hands in her lap. 'Good morning, Xavier. I hope you had a good night's sleep.'

She didn't exactly slouch, but she didn't sit straight up to attention like most of his employees did either. He couldn't say why, but that irritated him too.

As if she'd sensed his mood, she let a frown crease the smooth skin of her forehead. 'Jet lag?'

'Absolutely not.' He lifted his chin and stared down his nose. 'I spent two nights in Sydney before travelling north. That is more than enough time for a body to adjust to a new time zone.'

She pursed her lips and paused before speaking

again. 'You didn't work your way up from the bottom of the industry, did you?'

He wasn't sure what she was implying, but the criticism implicit in her words made his eyes narrow. 'You might want to be *very* careful what you say next, Miss Stephens.'

Instead of seeing her pale and straighten, he could've sworn the corners of her lips twitched.

'Would it help if I told you my middle name is Antonia?'

What on earth was she babbling about?

'You see, whenever I was in trouble my grandmother would call me *Wynne Antonia Stephens*.' She uttered her full name in deep, ominous tones. 'It occurs to me that you have the same aplomb to carry that off. Mind you, your "Miss Stephens" was suitably crushing. Though I should probably tell you that I prefer *Ms*.'

He leant towards her and the faint scent of coffee, bacon…and jasmine drifted across to him. 'What nonsense—you aren't the slightest bit crushed.'

She opened her eyes wide. 'Believe me, on the inside I'm utterly pulverised.'

It was all he could do to catch the smile that tried to slip free. She bit back a smile of her own and he suddenly found that his former irritation had drained away.

She clapped her hands together lightly. 'Now, you wanted to know about breakfasts…'

He listened as she told him that guests who

wanted breakfast needed to place their order and put it into the box on the reception desk by seven p.m. of the day before. Guests could choose to eat in the motel's drawing room or have room service. The menu was limited, but adequate. And it appeared that Wynne herself was the cook.

He made a note to inform Reyes of the system— if they wanted breakfast they would have to place their orders in a timely fashion.

'You have help.'

It wasn't a question. Someone had brought his tray up to his room this morning, and it hadn't been Wynne.

'I have a girl who comes in for three or four hours in the mornings when I need her.'

'What qualifications does she have?'

She blinked and very slowly straightened. 'What qualifications does she need? She delivers trays to the rooms and washes dishes.'

Her legs remained crossed, her hands remained folded in her lap, but Wynne Antonia Stephens was no longer relaxed.

He thought of the way she'd almost made him laugh a minute ago. If Lorenzo were to be believed, Aggie Stephens's charm had been lethal. Her granddaughter had obviously inherited it. However, while Lorenzo might have proved a pushover, his grandson was a very different proposition.

'She's hardworking, reliable and honest. In my eyes that makes her a model employee.'

'And are *you*?'

'A model employee?' She sat back. 'Hard to tell. I've been running this place for the last seven years. I've been the Chief rather than an Indian.'

Her eyes danced, but he refused to be beguiled by them again.

'I have no doubts whatsoever, though, that I've been a model boss.'

He didn't so much as crack a smile. 'I meant are you hardworking, reliable and honest?'

He watched the merriment fade from her eyes. He hadn't noticed how green they were till now, but perhaps it was simply a trick of the over-abundance of light pouring in at the windows.

'Are you impugning my character, *Mr* Ramos? Now that *is* something I'll take exception to.'

The *Mr Ramos* stung. He retaliated with, 'I did not appreciate being manipulated into employing you.'

'Ah…'

The martial light in her eyes faded. It was an unusual green—not emerald or sage. It shone with a softer and truer light—like jade.

'So that's why you're itching for a fight?'

The unadorned truth of her words found their target. Being here—*finally*—in this ludicrous second-rate motel, with its ridiculous charm, had torn the scabs off the anger and outrage that had been simmering since his grandfather's death. Now

that he was here he wanted to smash something…
or someone!

But Wynne—though she was *that woman's*
granddaughter—hadn't even been born when Aggie
had broken Lorenzo's heart, when she'd manipulated him and made him suffer. Xavier's heart might
burn with the injustice and heartbreak Lorenzo had
suffered, but in all likelihood Wynne had no idea
what had happened fifty-five years ago. He couldn't
blame her for it, or hold her responsible. And it
would be outrageous to punish her for it.

He straightened too, resisting the softening that
coursed through him. Wynne needed to understand
that *he* was in charge now. And the sooner he made
that clear the better.

'I'm planning to make changes here.'

'Of course you are. It's not like the place doesn't
need it.'

'I have no intention of fighting you every step of
the way or pandering to your sentimentality. You
either do the job I've employed you to do or you
hand your resignation in now.'

Her chin shot up, but it wasn't the sudden frost
in her eyes that Xavier noticed so much as the luscious curve of her bottom lip. He gazed at it, and
the longer he stared the harder and sharper the hunger that sliced through him. If he kissed her, would
that ice melt in the heat?

Her sharp, 'Yes, sir!' hauled him back.

The flush on her cheeks and the way she avoided

eye contact told him he'd been staring…and that it had made her uncomfortable.

He didn't want Wynne *comfortable*—he wanted her poised to carry out his every demand with flattering speed. He suspected if he gave the woman an inch she'd take a mile. But this was business, and he didn't want her feeling uncomfortable on a personal level.

'Do you have any other questions about how we run breakfast?'

'I'd like to create a breakfast room, where guests can help themselves to a buffet breakfast.'

'That would be lovely.' Her eyes said otherwise. 'But we don't have the equipment or the staff.'

'Yet.'

That perked her up.

He let her savour it. By the end of the day, when she'd had a taste of the wholesale changes he meant to make, he fully expected her unqualified resignation.

'The motel does not serve lunch or dinner?'

'No.'

Good. That meant he would have her full attention for the rest of the day. He started to rise.

'Well…' She grimaced. 'Not as a general rule.'

He sat again. 'Explain.'

'We get a lot of repeat business at Aggie's Retreat.'

'Yes?'

'That means we get to know our guests as…as individuals.'

She uttered that sentence as if it explained everything.

He stared at her. 'And?'

'So, for example, I know that Sandra Clark from up Cairns way would walk across hot coals for a halfway decent salmon cake, and that the favourite dish of Godfrey Trent from Sydney is crumbed cutlets.'

He gaped at her. 'You cook their favourite meals?'

'I charge through the nose for it.'

'How much?'

She told him and he shook his head. 'That's nothing compared to the majority of hotel restaurant rates.'

'But it's far more expensive than the Thai restaurant down the road or the tavern on the corner. I make a seventy per cent profit and the motel gets its guests' undying gratitude and loyalty. That sounds like a win-win, if you ask me.'

It made sound financial sense—except this wasn't the way the Ramos Corporation ran its hotels! 'What are you running here—a guesthouse? Because it certainly isn't a hotel.'

She suddenly smiled—one of *those* smiles. 'That's the perfect description. We're a home away from home. It's why our guests keep coming back.' Her smile widened. 'That and the fact that our rooms are so clean.'

'Which is just as well, as your rooms don't have anything else to recommend them.'

'Ouch. That's a little harsh. She's getting a little tired around the edges, I'll admit, but Aggie's Retreat still has charm.'

'*She's* shabby. And the charm is wearing thin.' He stabbed a finger to the table. 'I want a tour of the entire building. Now.'

'Rooms Three, Eight and Twelve won't be vacated until after ten, but the rest of the motel is at your disposal.'

He did his best to run her ragged for the next two hours, but she kept perfect pace with him. In any other circumstances he'd have been impressed, but not here. In fact the more time he spent in her company the more he realised she would have to go.

He couldn't fire her—he wouldn't stoop to that—but he'd be more than happy to accept her resignation once she handed it in. And he knew exactly how to achieve that.

He turned to her, cutting her off in mid-sentence as she told him some unpalatable truth or other about the building's ancient plumbing system. 'Wynne, I think it is time you learned the real reason I have bought Aggie's Retreat.'

'Excellent!' She rubbed her hands together. 'I've been wondering how long it would take you to put me out of my misery.'

His lips tightened. 'You do not look as if you are in any state of misery.' It looked as if misery were completely alien to this woman's existence. Unlike Lorenzo's. And unlike Xavier's own.

He pushed that last thought aside. He had no intention of descending into self-pity. Camilla might have proved as false as any woman could, but he had Luis. He would never regret his son. He'd come here to lay the ghosts of the past to rest—his grandfather's past and perhaps his own too. He would create a hotel that would do his grandfather proud. Maybe then both of them would have earned some peace.

Wynne tossed her head, and all her glorious hair bounced about her shoulders. Her smile only grew wider.

Dios, that smile!

'Allay my curiosity then.'

For no reason at all, his heart started to pound.

Those clear green eyes surveyed him, alive with curiosity and energy. 'After all, Aggie's Retreat isn't the kind of property the Ramos chain generally shows interest in.'

'That's because my interest in this establishment is personal.'

Her eyebrows lifted. 'Personal?'

She rubbed her hands together again, and for a moment all he could imagine was the feel of those hands on his bare flesh. Heat flooded him with a speed that had him sucking in a breath. He couldn't recall the last time thoughts of a woman, desire for a woman, had interfered with his work.

'Ooh, it sounds like there's a story here! I'm on the edge of my seat.'

No! He refused to want this woman.

He made his voice sharp. 'This story…it is *not* for your personal edification. I have no desire whatsoever to provide you with entertainment or amusement!'

The light in those lovely green eyes snapped off. 'No, of course not. I'm sorry.'

But even though she'd apologised, he had a feeling she'd prefer to stab him through the heart with something sharp and deadly. He could hardly blame her. She'd done nothing to deserve his rebuke. Her natural effervescence, however—her sense of fun, her attempts to be generous and pleasant—chafed at him. He didn't want her to be so congenial…so willing to approve of him…so *attractive*.

He didn't want to like her!

'The *"story"* as you so quaintly put it, is sordid and unpleasant, and it does your *grandmother* no credit!'

His teeth ground together. He had no right to tar Wynne with the same brush. If he were honest, he had no desire to hurt her either. He just wanted her…*gone*.

'This has something to do with Aggie?'

Her overly polite tone made him clench his teeth harder. He had no one to blame for that but himself.

Tell her the story, tell her what you mean to do,

*and then accept her resignation. Wish her well and
then you'll never have to see her again.*

Before he could start, however, she broke in. 'It
might be better to take this back to the conference
room, don't you think?'

He grew aware, then, of the rattling of the housekeeping cart in the hallway, and the fact that he
and Wynne were wedged in the bathroom of the
smallest room Aggie's Retreat had to offer. It was
a room Wynne didn't currently use, due to an issue
with the plumbing—the explanation of which he'd
cut short.

He gestured for her to precede him out of the
room. When they reached the conference room she
stood aside to let him enter first. She didn't take a
seat until he ordered her to sit. Her sudden deference had him grinding his back molars so hard he'd
need dental work by the time he returned to Spain.

Her face, when she turned to him, was smooth
and opaque and so formally courteous he had to
bite back another rebuke. What reprimand could
he utter? She was simply behaving in the manner
that he wanted her to—that he'd ordered her to. The
fact that he hated it was not her fault.

Aggie's past sins were not Wynne's fault either.
Even if she *had* unknowingly profited from them.

'You were about to explain why you'd purchased
Aggie's Retreat.'

Straight to the point. That, at least, he could appreciate.

'Did you know that Aggie won this establishment in a card game?'

'So that was the *truth*, then?' Luscious lips lifted as if they were unused to such rigorous restraint. They were garnered back under house arrest a moment later. 'I always thought it was a story my grandmother spun for dramatic impact. She was fond of a tall tale.'

'It was the truth.'

'I see.'

If she had any curiosity, she didn't show it. Xavier swallowed back the acid that burned his throat. 'My grandfather—Lorenzo Ramos—was the other card player. It was *his* hotel.'

'Ah.' She stared at him for a long moment. 'Was he in love with Aggie?'

His stomach clenched. 'Why do you say this?'

'When you're next in the foyer, look at the portrait on the wall behind the check-in desk. It's of Aggie when she was a young woman. She was very beautiful…and a free spirit in a time when that was unusual. She had a lot of admirers.'

Admirers? His grandfather hadn't simply been an *admirer*. He'd *loved* Aggie. And Aggie had taken advantage of that. She'd taken Lorenzo's heart and had run it through with her deceitful, conniving ways before tossing it aside as if it were…as if it were *nothing*!

And in his desolation and wretchedness Lorenzo had buckled to family pressure and married the

coldest woman Xavier had ever met—his grandmother. Lorenzo's heartbreak had led to the biggest mistake of his life, while Aggie had lived it
up with her ill-gotten gains. Was there no justice
in this world?

The smooth skin of Wynne's forehead creased.
'Has your grandfather held a grudge all these years?
Because she bested him in a card game?'

She clasped her hands on the table, and the in-
credulity in her eyes burned through him.

'Or is his grievance because he didn't win her
heart?'

'He held a grudge because your grandmother
cheated in that game of cards.' Xavier shot out
of his chair to pace the length of the room. 'This
motel should've been under the Ramos Corporation's aegis all these years.' He pointed a finger at
her. 'She manipulated him, made him fall in love
with her, and then she…*she cheated him.*'

He paced some more.

When she remained silent, he spun back. 'Are
you not going to say something?'

She lifted one slender shoulder. He couldn't
blame her for feeling at a loss. 'Your grandfather
told you all this?'

'On his deathbed.'

She stared, a frown gathering in her eyes.
'Xavier, when did your grandfather die?'

He had to breathe deeply in through his nose and

then let the breath out through his mouth before he could answer her. 'Not quite five weeks ago.'

For the briefest of moments her gaze softened. 'I'm sorry for your loss.'

He nodded. 'Thank you.'

A long silence ensued. All the while he was aware of her scrutiny. It was all he could do to feign indifference beneath it.

Finally she broke the quiet. 'So... He asked you to...?'

Xavier lifted his chin. 'Before he died he made me promise to buy the motel back.'

He had the penny piece and the Queen of Hearts card that Lorenzo had given him. He'd sworn to place them into Aggie's hand himself. Apparently Aggie would know what they signified. He didn't want to meet the woman who had caused his grandfather so much grief. But he had promised.

None of this is Wynne's fault.

He took his seat again, biting back a sigh. 'I am sorry if this gives you pain. I am sorry to be the one to reveal to you such an ugly truth about your grandmother.'

He waited for an outburst—protestations. Instead her gaze was removed from his as she stared down at the hands she'd pulled into her lap. From across the table he couldn't tell if they were clenched or not.

'You have nothing to say to this?'

'Um... Congratulations? You've won?'

He stiffened. 'I do not appreciate your flippancy.'

Her gaze lifted to his. She bit her lip, but it wasn't pain that threaded through those extraordinary eyes. It might almost be…pity!

'Oh, for heaven's sake, Xavier. You expect me to believe the ravings of a dying man? Seriously?'

His head rocked back.

'And then what? You want to turn this situation— *us*—into the Montagues and the Capulets? *Puh- lease!* I have better things to do with my time. And you should have too. One thing you *shouldn't* be doing is taking revenge for something your grand- father was too lazy to pursue himself while he was alive.'

'Too *lazy*…!'

He couldn't help but roar the words at her. He pushed himself and his chair away from the table, his stomach cramping as the pain of the loss of his grandfather pounded through him with renewed force.

'You know nothing about my grandfather! He was the kindest, most gentle of men, and he didn't deserve what Aggie did to him.'

'Have you ever noticed that when a man gets his heart broken it's always the woman's fault, but whenever a woman's heart is broken she's usually found at fault too?' She shot to her feet, hands on hips. 'You want to know what your sad little story tells me about your grandfather? That he was a fool risking his motel in a game of cards! What on earth was he *thinking*?'

A fool? Xavier clenched his hands so hard he started to shake.

'I also know that Lorenzo married and sired three sons. That doesn't exactly speak of heartbreak to me. And you needn't look so surprised. Did you expect me to do no homework on the Ramos Corporation? I know that Lorenzo founded a great hotel empire.'

Lorenzo had thrown himself into work because there'd been nothing for him at home. Not that Xavier had any intention of telling Wynne that.

'Which means he could've bought back Aggie's Retreat any time he wanted to while he was alive—if it was that important to him.

If? 'He had his pride!'

Her jaw dropped, but her shock was far from edifying.

'If he truly loved Aggie, but let *pride* prevent him from pursuing her, then…then he deserved his broken heart.'

'You're as heartless as your grandmother!'

She closed her eyes and dragged in a breath. 'I'm just pointing out that you know only one side of the story. I can tell you right now that Aggie enjoyed male attention. She never made any secret of it. I can also tell you, with my hand pressed to my heart, that she would never have cheated in a matter of honour. But as you don't know her I don't expect you to believe me. And here's a novel thought for you, Xavier. What happened between Aggie and Lorenzo has absolutely *nothing* to do with us—it's none of our business. And I have absolutely no intention of troubling myself with it further.'

The burning in his chest intensified. 'You do not love your grandmother?'

'On the contrary—I adore her.'

'But you do not care that I mean to obliterate every trace of Aggie—*your beloved grandmother*—from this motel?'

Her brow wrinkled and she leaned towards him. 'Xavier, Aggie resides in the hearts of all those who love her—in my heart, my mother's heart… Lorenzo's heart. This—' she gestured around the conference room, presumably to encompass the whole motel '—when you get right down to it, is nothing more than an old pile of cold bricks.'

The woman didn't have a sentimental bone in her body! It didn't give her the right, though, to make him feel guilty or…or *juvenile* for trying to right a past wrong.

Xavier lifted his jaw at just *that* angle—full of imperious arrogance—that made her want to slug him.

'I'm willing to accept your resignation any time you wish to proffer it, Miss Stephens.'

'It's *Ms*. Also, you left out the "Wynne Antonia". I promise you the full name carries more weight.'

He glared at her, but before he could open his mouth and fire her she continued.

'I have no intention of proffering my resignation. I knew you would make changes to the motel. I have no issue with that. Some changes are long overdue. As for the history between our grandparents—as I've said, I have no intention of concerning myself with it. As far as I'm concerned nothing has changed.'

Xavier's glare deepened, but April chose that moment to appear in the doorway.

Wynne stood and excused herself.

'This had better be important,' she murmured to the other woman.

April nodded, and as Wynne listened to what she had to say her stomach started to knot.

She swung back to Xavier briefly. 'I'm sorry, but there's a situation I need to deal with.'

Irritation flitted across his face. 'Can't you get—?'

'No, I can't.'

There was no time to stand around arguing. She took off down the corridor to Room Twelve. Ignoring the *Do Not Disturb* sign on the door, she knocked. 'Ms Gladstone?' She knocked harder. 'Serena?'

No answer.

Without further ado Wynne swiped her master key and pushed through the door. The breath caught in her throat when she saw Serena crumpled on the floor.

'April, call for an ambulance immediately.' She

raced over to kneel beside the unconscious woman, reaching for her hand. 'Let them know she's diabetic and twelve weeks pregnant.'

CHAPTER THREE

WYNNE'S FINGERS SHOOK, but she found Serena's pulse. *Thank you, God!* It was faint, though, and that couldn't be good. She chafed one cold hand between both of her own.

'Serena… Serena, honey, can you hear me?'

Serena didn't stir.

And then she was aware of Xavier, kneeling beside her, taking Serena's other hand.

'*Dios!* She is freezing.'

She hadn't realised he'd followed her. He'd probably meant to fire her once he'd caught up with her, for insubordination. He still might.

He made as if to lift the unconscious woman, but Wynne stopped him. 'I'm not sure we should move her.'

She was pregnant. What if they accidentally did something to hurt both Serena and the baby?

Without a word, he pulled the quilt from the bed and tucked it around the woman with such gentleness it had a lump forming in Wynne's throat.

'What else can I do?'

She swallowed. 'Can you hold her hand?'

Shocked dark eyes met hers. 'She knows you, yes?'

She nodded.

'If she regains consciousness a familiar face will be a comfort to her.'

That was true, but in that case what she was about to ask him to do was far from glamorous.

'Tell me,' he ordered.

She wondered briefly if the man even knew how to couch his demands as requests. She shook the thought off. They had far more important things to consider at the moment.

'Can you check the bathroom for any signs of vomit or…' she swallowed '…blood?'

He didn't even blink—just set off to do her bidding at once.

He returned a moment later. 'Vomit, but no blood.'

That meant Serena hadn't lost the baby.

Yet.

'We need to let the paramedics know that when they arrive.'

April appeared in the doorway. 'The ambulance is on its way. Tina is primed to show them up here the moment they arrive. They're less than five minutes away. Is there anything else you'd like me to do?' She sent a covert glance in Xavier's direction. 'Or would you like me to…get on with things?'

Dear Lord. If Libby or the other housemaids got wind of this there'd be tears before bedtime.

'Thanks, April. If you can just…keep things as normal as possible for the rest of the staff and guests, that would be great. And, if we can manage it, I'd like as few sightseers as possible. It's our responsibility to safeguard Ms Gladstone's privacy.'

'I'll do everything I can,' April promised, closing the door behind her.

Wynne glanced back down at Serena, gently pushing the hair from her face. 'Serena, honey, can you hear me? Give my hand a squeeze if you can.'

Nothing.

In the next moment a damp washcloth was pushed into her hand, and she wasn't sure why but the large solid shape of Xavier in the room helped to steady her. She gently pressed the washcloth to Serena's brow, and then her cheeks, murmuring to the other woman the entire time—telling her where she was and what they were doing, saying anything she could think of to reassure her.

She glanced up briefly. 'Xavier, could you check the dishes on the sideboard—' she nodded in its direction '—and tell me what food is there? I want to know if she's eaten this morning.'

He strode across with long, assured strides and the more she looked at him the steadier her pulse became.

'One rasher of bacon, two eggs, two pieces of toast.'

He glanced back at her with his eyebrows raised.

She sent him a weak smile. 'So that means she's eaten one rasher of bacon and the beans.'

He lifted up some orange peel. 'And an orange. This we must tell to the paramedics too, yes?'

She nodded, and beneath the quilt Serena stirred.

'The ambulance is here,' Xavier murmured from the window that overlooked the front of the motel.

Excellent.

'Hey, honey.' Wynne found a smile as Serena opened her eyes. 'It's good to have you back with us.'

Serena blinked and frowned, glanced about, and then her hand clutched Wynne's. 'The baby?' she croaked.

Wynne gave her hand a reassuring squeeze. 'Now, don't you go upsetting yourself. There's absolutely no indication of any kind that there's anything wrong with your baby. And look—' She tried to stand as the paramedics entered the room, but the other woman refused to relinquish her hand. 'The ambulance crew is here, and they'll take excellent care of you. They'll take you to hospital and the doctors will give you a thorough check to make sure everything is okay. You'll see. Everything will be fine.'

Fear flitted across Serena's face and she struggled to rise. 'Please don't leave me, Wynne.' She coughed as if she had a dry throat. 'Please, I—'

The entreaty in the other woman's eyes twisted Wynne's heart. 'I'll come with you.' She squeezed her hand. 'And I'll call your sister. You don't worry about anything—you hear? You just concentrate on feeling better.'

Serena subsided with a nod. 'Bless you, Wynne…'

The paramedics allowed Wynne to ride in the ambulance.

Before they left, Xavier pushed Serena's handbag into Wynne's arms. 'You'll probably need her details. And her phone to find her sister's number.'

His quick thinking surprised her. 'Thank you.'

'I'll take care of everything that needs doing from this end.'

Would he even know what to do? She let that thought slide as the ambulance doors closed. She didn't want to leave him alone with her staff, but she had no choice. Between them Tina and April would take care of everything…keep the ship afloat.

She crossed her fingers. Crossed them for Serena, for all her staff, and for herself.

Wynne planted herself on a bench in the anonymous hospital waiting room. She waited. And waited. She rang Serena's sister, who lived two hours away. She made the other woman promise to drive safely. She made her promise to take a ten-minute break at the halfway point in her journey.

She glanced at her watch. She'd only been here for thirty minutes, but the minutes seemed like hours. The medical staff told her that Serena was in a stable condition, but they refused to tell her anything else…such as whether Serena had lost her baby or not.

Her stomach churned. *Let the baby be okay.*

Serena wanted that baby with every fibre of her being. If she lost it—

Don't even think that.

She started when a plastic cup was pushed underneath her nose. She took it automatically, and stared in astonishment as Xavier folded himself down on to the padded bench beside her, holding another cup.

'Tea,' he said. 'I thought you might like one.'

She blinked, but he didn't disappear. 'What… what are you doing here?'

'I brought Ms Gladstone's things. We thought she might need them.'

She nodded, and then glanced around.

'I left them at the nurses' station.'

'Oh, good thinking.'

He frowned, and leaned forward to peer at her. He smelled like vanilla and pinecones and the sea—all her favourite things.

'Wynne, are you okay?'

She suddenly realised she'd been staring, but not talking. She shook herself. 'I'm fine. Just worried about Serena.'

His frown deepened. Gone was all his former arrogance and…and *hardness*. In its place…

In its place was concern and warmth and something else she couldn't quite pin down—but it made her stomach curl and warmed the toes she hadn't even realised were cold.

'The nurse has informed me that she is in a stable condition.'

Oh, that accent! When he wasn't playing the role of demanding boss or avenging angel… A shiver rippled through her. Yes, that accent could do the strangest things to a woman's insides.

'So why all this worry?'

She leapt up to stride across the room. 'Because that's all they've told me too!' She strode back again. 'What they *haven't* told me is if her baby is all right.'

He stared up at her, but she couldn't read his expression.

Very gently he pulled her back down beside him. 'Yes, I can see why that would be important. I will make a deal with you, Ms Wynne Antonia Stephens.'

He didn't use an ominous tone, and the way his mouth shaped her full name, with the smallest of smiles playing across his lips, made her pulse race.

'A deal?'

'The minute you finish your cup of tea I will go and find out all I can about Serena and her baby.'

She stared at him, liking this new, improved version of her boss. But… 'What makes you think they'll tell *you* anything?'

He raised a supercilious eyebrow and she found herself having to choke back a laugh. This was a man used to getting his own way. Tomorrow that might be devastating. Today, however, it would be useful—very useful.

She pulled the lid off her cup. 'Xavier Mateo Ramos, you have yourself a deal.'

When she smiled at him he smiled back, and the day didn't seem so bleak and dark. Somewhere a ray of hope shone amid the dark gloom of worry.

'You must not gulp it down in one go,' he ordered. 'It will be very hot.'

And sweet. She tried not to grimace as she took her first sip. Maybe he thought she needed sweetening. She thought back over their conversation in the conference room earlier and conceded that he might have a point. She really needed to work on her deference and being tactful skills.

She bit back a sigh and took another sip of her tea. 'I'm sorry, Xavier. This isn't what I had planned for your first day.'

'It is not your fault.' He eyed her thoughtfully. 'You were quite amazing, you know—very calm and collected.'

She'd felt like jelly inside. 'So were you.'

'But you knew what to do. I did not.'

She'd bet that didn't happen very often. It wouldn't be particularly tactful to point that out, though. Still, it was nice to have some evidence that he wasn't totally invulnerable.

'Serena is one of our regulars, so I know her situation.'

'Her diabetes and her pregnancy?'

Her heart started to pound again. *Please let Serena's baby be safe.*

'Tell me your procedure in such cases. You obviously have one.'

'Cases like this are rare, thankfully.'

'Why did April come and get you? She must clean occupied rooms all the time.'

'We have a policy that if the *Do Not Disturb* sign is on the door for too long two staff members should be present when entering the room.' And, given April's criminal record, Wynne had no intention of placing her housekeeping manager in a potentially compromising situation.

Xavier nodded slowly. 'Yes. I can see how that would be wise.'

'April had Tina ring through to the room first, but when there was no answer…'

'She came and got you?'

Wynne nodded.

He stared at her, a frown in his eyes. 'I do not understand why April was concerned enough to raise the alarm.'

Oh. 'Like I said, Serena is a regular. She's a hair and make-up artist and she was in the Gold Coast for a fashion show yesterday—she does a lot of them. She normally checks out at ten on the dot. She'd made no other changes to her usual routine— her breakfast was delivered at seven-thirty—and as it was after eleven…'

'So…' Xavier pursed his lips. 'You choose to risk invoking your clients' wrath—which you might have done if Serena Gladstone had simply been seeking quiet and solitude—in the interests of ensuring their wellbeing?'

That was a no-brainer! 'Yes.'

He leant back and sipped his tea. 'It is lucky for Serena that you chose the less professional option.'

Was he criticising her? He couldn't be serious?

Bite your tongue, Wynne Antonia Stephens. Pick your battles.

'How long would *you* have left it?' She tried to keep the accusation out of her voice.

'I hire staff to make those decisions for me.'

Do you feel safe and smug, tucked up in that ivory tower of yours?

She bit her tongue until she tasted blood. She wanted to bring this conversation to a close. *Now.* She lifted her cup and drained the rest of the awful tea. Oddly, though, both the liquid and the sugar had made her feel better.

She handed him her cup. 'I've kept my side of the deal.'

His eyes throbbed into hers, but without a word her rose and left—presumably to find out all he could about Serena's condition.

Wynne couldn't endure sitting for another moment. She paced the waiting room, hoping the activity would help allay the tension that had her coiling up tighter by the second. In her mind's eye, all she could see was the excitement stretching across Serena's face last night as she'd told Wynne all her plans for the baby.

It had made Wynne almost...*jealous.*

Xavier was gone for twenty minutes.

Wynne paced the waiting room. *Please. Please. Please.* That one word went round and round in her head like a prayer. There would not be enough comfort in the world for Serena if she lost her baby.

For no reason, all the hairs on her arms lifted. She spun to find Xavier standing in the doorway. Her mouth went dry.

'Well?' She couldn't manage anything above a whisper.

'At the moment the doctor is optimistic that both Serena and her baby will be okay. Serena may need bed-rest for the remainder of her pregnancy, but...'

Xavier continued, but Wynne barely heard the rest of his words. She just let them wash over her in a comforting rush. She dropped down to one of the padded benches that lined the walls, the strength in her legs giving way.

'Oh, Xavier.' She pressed both hands to her chest. 'That's great news.'

And to her utter embarrassment she burst into tears.

In two strides he was across the room. A warm arm went about her shoulders, a strong thigh pressed against hers as he took the seat beside her. From shoulder to knee she found herself held against him—he was warm and solid and comforting, and she drew all of that in as she hauled a breath into shuddering lungs and wrangled her emotions back under control.

'I'm sorry. I know this isn't very *professional* of me, but…'

'But it has been a harrowing morning and it has ended better than you feared. Wynne, your tears are entirely understandable.'

Really?

'Come.'

He smiled, and she couldn't find a trace of criticism in those dark eyes of his.

'It is time I took you home.'

Her heart clenched. She wasn't sure she even *had* a home any more.

'I promised Serena's sister I'd wait here till she arrived.'

He settled back with a nod.

Shock had her straightening. 'You don't have to stay, Xavier.'

He briefly clasped her hand, and heat flooded her. His eyes speared hers and she felt suspended between breaths. And then he edged away slightly, and the tightness about her chest eased a fraction.

'I'll wait.'

She wasn't sure she wanted him to. But nevertheless she found his presence comforting. She told herself it was because while he was here with her he wasn't at Aggie's Retreat unsupervised, finding fault with things without her there to explain them *in context*. But the truth was that she simply appreciated the company.

She swallowed. It was the same way she'd have appreciated Tina or April's company. Except…

She couldn't remember Tina or April ever sending unexpected jolts of adrenaline coursing through her and reminding her of what it was like to feel alive—truly alive—rather than worried about everything and running around trying to put out fires.

For the moment, she decided to put the thought of fires and catastrophes out of her mind and simply enjoy the opportunity for some peace and quiet.

'This isn't the way back to the motel.'

Xavier glanced across at Wynne. 'I've instructed Reyes to take us to an Oceanside restaurant. You haven't had lunch and it is after two. You need to eat.'

She glanced at her watch, and although he had a feeling that she wanted to argue with him, she subsided back against the upholstery of the limousine. She barely seemed to notice the luxury of the large car, but he appreciated the leather seats after spending so long on those hard hospital benches.

Wynne must be worn out. *He* felt drained and he'd done next to nothing.

'I have it on good authority that Clementine's is an excellent restaurant.'

'Yes, the reviews have been admirable.'

He frowned as the car came to halt in front of one of the Gold Coast's most exciting new restaurants and Wynne showed not the slightest interest or excitement. He'd wanted to give her a treat for all her quick thinking and kindness to Serena Gladstone, but it appeared this wasn't the kind of excursion designed to bring a smile to Wynne's lips.

'You would rather eat somewhere else?'

She sent him a look that he found difficult to interpret. 'I'd be just as happy with hot chips on the beach.' She glanced down at his feet. 'But you're not dressed for the beach.'

He too glanced down at his Italian leather shoes and silk blend socks. Before he could stop the words coming out of his mouth he said, 'That can be fixed. I can take them off.'

She stared at him with so much surprise that he reached down and removed them at once. He met her gaze, defiance threading through him, and raised a deliberately challenging eyebrow. After two beats she gave a laugh and kicked off her own shoes. To see the effervescence and energy return to her eyes was the only reward he needed.

He bought two cones of chips and they ambled along the beach before finding a spot to sit where they could dig their toes into the sand. The beach—all golden sand and blue skies—stretched for miles in both directions, with the Gold Coast skyline stretching behind—mile upon mile of glamorous high-rises. The lightest of breezes touched his face, bringing with it the scent of salt and jasmine— the former from the ocean and the latter from the woman sitting beside him.

'I want to tell you again that I think you did an extraordinary job today.'

She frowned. 'You mean I was supposed to take your earlier criticism as a *compliment*?'

He stiffened. 'What criticism?'

'That by ignoring the *Do Not Disturb* sign I was being unprofessional.'

He glared at her. 'That is not what I meant!'

She shrugged and stared back out at the surf. 'It's what you said.'

He found himself wrestling with a sudden anger. He was her employer. He didn't need to explain himself to her.

Except...except if he'd given her the impression that he'd been criticising her then perhaps he did.

'I am sorry if I gave you that impression.' His words came out stiff, and he could have sworn out loud when her jaw tightened. 'What I was trying to say was that I admire your understanding of your clients and your attention to their needs. I admire your...vigilance.'

She turned back to him, the smallest of frowns lurking in the depths of her eyes. 'I work in a people profession. I'm trained to anticipate people's needs.'

'I work in a people profession too.'

A laugh shot out of her and she immediately tried to smother it. 'We may work in the same industry, but we're worlds apart, Xavier—and I'm not just talking about Northern and Southern hemispheres, here. You're not the least interested in anticipating anyone's needs. You hire staff for that. What *you're* used to is barking out orders and having them obeyed immediately and without question.'

The moment the words left her she winced, her shoulders edging up towards her ears. 'I didn't mean that to sound disrespectful. I just meant we play different roles on the hotel industry's food chain.'

He believed her—that she hadn't meant to offend him. But in that moment he realised how distant, how remote he was from the day-to-day running of his hotels. He couldn't be remote from this one. It meant too much.

His heart started to pound. 'That's what you meant when you said earlier that I had clearly not worked my way up from the bottom?'

She eyed him warily and nodded.

'And you do not like it?'

She glanced away again with a shake of her head that he couldn't interpret. Her lips remained firmly closed. They'd both abandoned any pretence of eating their chips.

Something inside him clenched. He pushed his shoulders back. 'I would prefer you to speak your mind.'

Her chin lifted. 'Would you? But if I speak my mind it might give you the reason you're looking for to give me the old heave-ho?'

'Heave-ho?'

'Fire me,' she explained.

'Ah, no.' He shook his head. 'I cannot dismiss

you for anything you say now. Not on a day when you have been a heroine. You are aware, are you not, that you may have in fact saved Serena Gladstone's life?'

Her mouth dropped open.

'And I will not dismiss you for being honest when I have *asked* you to be honest. That would be dishonourable.'

He followed the bob of her throat as she swallowed. The long clean line of her neck and the warm glow of her skin filtered into his consciousness, and an itch started up deep inside of him. He did his best to ignore it.

She pressed her hands together and cleared her throat. 'Mr Ramos—'

'Xavier,' he ordered.

Her chest rose and fell. He had a feeling that she was counting to three before she spoke again.

'Xavier, you've made no secret of the fact that you don't like me.'

He opened his mouth, but she held up a hand and he closed it again.

'I understand personality clashes—they're a fact of life—but that shouldn't mean we can't work together. That's why manners are so important. They grease the wheels, so to speak, and keep us all civilised. But you've made no attempt at politeness. *That's* what my earlier comment referred to. If you'd had to work your way up from the bottom you would have more…'

'More…?' The word emerged on a croak.

She swallowed. 'You would have a greater respect for the feelings of others and the impression you make on them.'

The vein at his temple throbbed. 'You think I do not care for the feelings of others?'

He thought back over all their dealings so far—the way he had spoken to her, treated her—and he wanted to close his eyes and swear loud and long. He had been acting like a bear with the proverbial sore head. While she…she had been busy saving a guest's life! She'd treated him with kindness and friendliness, and in return…

She deserved better from him. *Much* better.

She deserved an explanation.

It took him a moment before he trusted his voice not to betray him. 'I do not dislike you, Wynne. It is true, though, that I have been very short with you. That is because I have been expecting opposition from you in relation to the changes I mean to implement at Aggie's Retreat.' It took an effort of will not to drag a hand down his face and betray how weary he was. 'I should have given you the benefit of the doubt. My behaviour has been very rude. I am sorry.'

Again, the shock in her eyes was not edifying.

She deserves an honest explanation.

A weight slammed down on him and his shoulders sagged. Pained scored through his chest. 'My grief for my grandfather is still very raw and… How do you say it? I have been using you as my whipping boy, yes?'

She nodded.

'It has been very unfair of me. It is obvious that I should've waited longer before coming here to the Gold Coast.'

Dear God, the *pain* in Xavier's eyes! Wynne had to swallow and blink hard. He must have loved his grandfather very much.

She refused to voice that thought, though. He hadn't appreciated any of her attempts at friendliness so far today, and she suspected any prying on her part would be rebuffed...sternly. Even after his heartfelt apology. And it *had* been heartfelt.

His revelation of the reason why he'd bought Aggie's Retreat still shocked her to the soles of her feet. His grief she understood—but his anger... That anger felt far too personal, and she didn't want to be subjected to it again.

And yet here on the beach in the bright afternoon sunlight it wasn't Xavier's earlier anger that held her attention, but the fact that his eyes weren't as jet-black as she'd originally thought. She glanced at them again, just to double-check. They were the colour of dark chocolate...and they had the same shine as melted chocolate. She glanced briefly at his lips and then forced her gaze away.

'Am I forgiven?'

His voice made her start. 'Of course you're forgiven, Xavier. I—' How did she put this tactfully? 'You…?'

Tact be damned—she went with her heart instead. 'I'm really sorry that your grandfather is no longer with us.' It was all she could do not to reach out and clasp his hand. 'I'm sorry that you miss him so much. But your love and loyalty are a beautiful testimony. You make me wish that I could've known him.'

He stared at her, and then he sent her one of his rare smiles. It did the craziest things to her pulse. *Stop it!*

'Thank you, Wynne.'

She hoped her shrug oozed composure. 'I can understand how the initial shock of being here must've…thrown you.'

Please God, don't let him interpret that as being too personal.

She dusted off her hands and did her best to look businesslike. 'But the fact of the matter is that you *are* here in Surfers Paradise, and…and surely we should be able to work together in professional manner— especially now we've been so honest with each other.'

'I expect you are right.'

He didn't look convinced. She soldiered on anyway. She owed it to Tina, April, Meg and Libby… all of her other workers…to stick this out for as long as she could. At least until she could guarantee that their jobs were safe.

'It is in my remit to make your job here easier, Xavier, not harder. I take that duty seriously.'

He frowned, though not at her, which gave her heart.

She found a smile. 'And tomorrow, as they say, is another day. Let's hope it's not quite as dramatic.'

'Amen!'

'Oh, and before I forget—I've been meaning to mention that while you're here I'd be happy to make an evening meal for us all.'

He turned to her, his eyes blank. 'Who do you mean by *us all*?'

'You, Reyes and myself…your son and his nanny when they arrive…and any guests who'd like to join us.' She hesitated when he didn't answer. 'I'm not your chef, Xavier, or your maid, so I'm not offering to cook you a meal to serve to you in your room. If you prefer to cook for yourself, or to hire a chef, the kitchen is, of course, at your disposal.'

His chin came up. 'I would not ask you to act either as my chef or my maid. I do not doubt that you work hard enough as it is, without adding those jobs to your list of duties.' He stared at her for several long moments. 'You are really offering to cook for me?'

She swallowed at his surprise…and at how intimate the arrangement sounded.

'You and everyone else.' She made her voice deliberately crisp in an effort to shake off the warm languor that tried to steal over her. 'I cook an evening meal for myself. It won't take much extra effort to cook for a few more. It's the hospitable thing to do, and Aggie's Retreat prides itself on its hospitality.'

'I would be pleased to accept your offer. It's very kind of you.'

She blinked, his warmth surprising her. 'I do have one rule.' Not that she was in any position to be making rules, but…

He tensed. 'Which is…?'

'There's to be no work discussions during dinnertime. Dinner is for relaxation and enjoying good food.'

The tension melted from his shoulders. The smile he sent her nearly melted her to the spot.

'Agreed.'

She crossed her fingers. Maybe the two of them would find some common ground. Maybe she'd find a way to stop him from smashing her poor little motor inn to smithereens.

CHAPTER FOUR

'SO, AS YOU can see…' Wynne gestured to the fence line that separated her little cottage from Aggie's Retreat '…the motel property boundary comes to here.'

They stood in the western corner at the rear of the property. He pointed to her home. 'What's that?'

It was almost impossible not to tease him. 'I'm pretty certain you don't want me to answer *a house* to that question.'

His lips didn't soften. Nor did the determination that made his eyes so dark and intense. He flicked an unimpressed glance in her direction. 'You would be correct.'

She bit back a sigh. The glimpses she'd caught yesterday of the grief-stricken grandson, the considerate man who hadn't resented the time she'd taken to look after Serena, were gone today.

And yet the memory of his grief—the raw pain that had yawned through his eyes—was burned onto her memory. That man might be nowhere in sight at the moment, but she knew he was in there somewhere—lurking beneath the surface, grieving—and she ached to reach him.

'It is a private residence, yes?'

She snapped to attention at his barked question. 'Yes.'

'Who owns it?'

'I do.'

He stilled, and then he spun to her. 'I want to buy it. I want that land.'

She took a step away from him, her chest tightening so hard her lungs hurt. 'It's not for sale.'

That was her home!

He drummed his fingers against his thigh—a strong and powerful thigh. She stared at those fingers, at that thigh, and swallowed. With a superhuman effort she forced her gaze back to his face, but a buzzing had taken up residence in her blood—a buzzing that soon became a raw, aching need that recognised and relished the strong lean lines of the man in front of her, the broad shoulders, the firm lips…the hot masculine aura that seemed to call to her.

What on earth was wrong with her? *Remember what he wants to do*! *Remember what he thinks of Aggie!*

She forced her gaze back to her house. 'It's not for sale,' she repeated.

'I would make it worth your while.'

He was talking about money, but money couldn't buy her what that little cottage represented—security, a home, cherished memories.

You could use it as a bargaining chip.

She reached out to steady herself against the fence. Would she sell her cottage if it would ensure her staff kept their jobs?

In a heartbeat.

But the thought had tears burning the backs of her eyes.

'I…' She swallowed. 'Can we discuss this another time? I…it's not something I'd ever considered.'

'As you wish.'

Ha, that was laughable! Nothing was as she wished.

Pulling herself together and feigning indifference, she pointed to the roof of the motel. 'From here you can see quite clearly that we need new guttering.'

He followed her finger. 'From here it looks as if the entire roof needs replacing.'

'There's a reason you got Aggie's Retreat at such a bargain basement price.'

His snort told her what he thought of that.

She opened the gate in the fence as Tina's six-year-old twins came racing across from the motel. 'Hi, boys, have you met Mr Ramos yet?'

'Hello, Mr Ramos,' they sing-songed.

'Xavier, this is Blake and Heath—Tina's sons.'

'We're going to play cricket,' Blake said, as both boys shot into her backyard.

She glanced at Xavier, who stared after them bemused. 'They have great plans to teach your Luis how to play cricket.'

Stunned dark eyes met hers. 'Luis?'

'But of course. I told you we do a mighty fine welcome here at Aggie's Retreat.' She grinned up at him. 'Playmates for the boss's son at no extra cost.'

'They...they play here every day?'

'Every school day.'

'You run a crèche as well as a guest house?'

She folded her arms. 'I do what I can to keep my staff happy. I employ good people and I want to keep them. Letting Heath and Blake play in my backyard for an hour or so till Tina's shift ends is no skin off anyone's nose.'

He shook his head. 'This expression I do not know.'

Oh. 'Um... I simply mean the arrangement doesn't hurt anyone...and it does some good. Why wouldn't I choose an option that ticks those boxes?'

He didn't say anything.

She folded her arms. 'They're nice boys.'

'I'm sure they are.'

She waited, but he didn't add anything.

He rolled his shoulders and glared. 'Why are you looking at me like this?' he burst out.

'Thank you, Wynne, for thinking of my son...?'

'I...'

A breath huffed out of her. She couldn't stop it. 'Your suspicion is insulting. We do not have dastardly designs on Luis.'

He drew himself up to his full imposing height. 'I never for a moment thought you did.'

She wanted to call him a liar.

Bite your tongue. Pick your battles. You have bigger fish to fry.

His eyes flashed. 'I have phone calls to make and business to attend to.'

With a roll of her eyes that she made sure he didn't see she started back across the asphalt of the overflow parking area and punched in the security code for the motel's back door.

There were two staircases that accessed the upper floors—this one, and the one in the foyer. The conference room was located at the top of this set of stairs, with Xavier's rooms stretching beyond it.

When she reached the landing at the top she saluted a painting on the wall. 'Afternoon, Captain.'

Xavier halted in front of the painting. 'What are you doing?'

'I'm going to write you a report.'

'I mean this.' He gestured to the painting. 'Why do you talk to it?'

She moved back. The old-time sea captain with his beard, pipe and the roguish twinkle in his eye beamed down at her. 'I always salute the Captain. I have since I was a little girl. Some of the guests do too. We have no idea who he is, so we make up stories about him. It's just a bit of whimsy that everyone seems to enjoy.'

'He is...' His lip curled. 'This painting is clichéd and poorly executed. It has to go.'

She'd started to move towards the conference room, but she swung back at that. 'You can't get rid of the Captain! You'll have a mutiny on your hands.'

His eyes narrowed. 'I appreciate all you've done since my arrival, and I appreciate the fact that you've kept my son in your thoughts, but that doesn't change the reason why I'm here or what I mean to do. If I haven't made it clear enough already, let me do so now—this is *my* motel.'

His jaw tightened, but that didn't hide the pain that she saw flash momentarily through his eyes.

'As such, I can do with *my* motel whatever I like.'

He had a point. And she should want to punch him on the nose for pointing it out with such brutal bluntness, except...

Xavier slashed a hand through the air, but it didn't hide the ache still stretching through his eyes. 'Lorenzo deserves better than this!'

She pressed a hand to her chest. He must have loved his grandfather dearly. Yesterday she'd been granted a glimpse beneath Xavier's steely façade, and rather than simmering aggression what she'd seen had been grief. God only knew she understood grief—understood how it could eat at you from the inside out, lie dormant for days and then rear up its head to spit poison at you from every direction.

She moved back towards him. He stood a step below her, which almost made them eye to eye. And for a moment she saw the pain she'd witnessed yesterday. She'd never been able to turn away from the wounded or the wretched.

'You must miss Lorenzo so very much.'

His nostrils flared. His Adam's apple bobbed.

She couldn't stop herself from pressing her hand to his cheek. 'I'm sorry that being here has made that wound so raw, Xavier.'

He reached up and removed her hand. She readied herself for some crushing set-down about inappropriate familiarity, but his touch was gentle, and his thumb ran back and forth across the sensitive skin of her inner wrist, sending a hypnotic but demanding heat spiralling through her.

His gaze lowered to her lips and his eyes turned smoky and heavy-lidded. He leaned towards her and her breath hitched. Surely he didn't mean to kiss her? She shouldn't be standing here as if…as if she were waiting for him to do exactly that!

'What kind of comfort are you offering me, Wynne?'

His voice was low and seductive. His breath fanned across her lips, teasing them, sensitising them. The smoky accent heated something low down in her abdomen. Tendrils of temptation curled through her until she pulsed with need and heat, aching in places she'd forgotten she had. All she had to do was lean forward and she would know what this man tasted like. One kiss and…

She glanced up into his eyes. The cold, calculated hardness in them—so at odds with his touch and his words—made her shrink back inside herself.

She took a step away from him, tugging her hand free. 'Not that kind of comfort.'

Her voice sounded as if it belonged to somebody else.

'Are you sure?'

How could he make his voice so warm when his eyes were so hard?

'Positive.'

'Because I do not fraternise with my staff.'

She prickled at the threat latent in his words—that if she attempted to *fraternise* with him he'd see it as grounds for instant dismissal. She couldn't be dismissed. Not yet.

She drew herself up to her full height. 'If by *fraternise* you mean sleep with, then let me assure you that you're safe from me.' She whirled around and made for the conference room. 'You're not my type,' she hurled over her shoulder.

She'd been told once before that she wasn't *good* enough—not polished enough, first-rate enough, sophisticated enough to move in the exalted circles the very rich and the very talented moved in. Xavier moved in even more exalted circles than Duncan, and she had no intention of setting herself up to be told *again* that she didn't measure up. *No way, José!*

'Not your type?'

He roared the words at her back, and she didn't know why her assertion should upset him. Maybe he was just grumpy because his ploy hadn't worked.

She swung around when she reached the far side of the conference table. He stood framed in the doorway like some clichéd Greek god.

'I don't believe for a single moment that I've dented your fragile male ego. I don't believe there's a single fragile thing about you.'

Deference, Wynne! You're supposed to be practising deference.

But the rotten man had all but sent her a heated invitation with the sole purpose of trapping her in inappropriate conduct. So he could fire her. And she'd almost fallen for it!

She folded her arms. 'Admittedly, you're attractive…'

Only an idiot would claim otherwise, and despite everything she wasn't an idiot.

He glared at her, and bit by bit her sense of humour righted itself.

'But then so am I.'

When she wanted it, she never lacked for male company. It was just that these days she didn't seem to want it. The motel and her grandmother took all her energy. Whatever was left was reserved for hunkering down with a bowl of popcorn and watching old movies.

She shook herself, wishing she could just as easily shake away the bad feeling that had developed between them. She didn't want him taking out his resentment of her on the rest of the staff—she had to make sure that didn't happen. So she set about making amends.

'The simple fact of the matter is you're too successful for my taste, Xavier.'

He moved into the room. He rolled his shoulders. 'What does your taste normally run to?'

Lifting the lid of her laptop, she planted herself behind it. 'I seem to attract…artistic types.'

He rocked back on his heels. She had a feeling he was trying hard not to let his lip curl.

She nodded once—hard. 'Yes, artistic types… Which is a flattering term that, from my experience, few of them have earned.' She slanted a glance up at him, trying hard not to laugh—though laughing would be better than crying. 'You can translate that to mean that they don't have jobs…nor any prospects on the horizon.'

She opened a new document. 'Synonyms for "artistic type" might also include wastrel, layabout and slob. My personal favourite term, however, is no-hope loser. Hence *my type*, Xavier, is no-hope loser. *You* cannot be described as a no-hope loser in anybody's language. So, you see, you're quite safe.'

He sat, spreading his hands with an expansive and what she thought must be a typically Mediterranean eloquence that made her abdomen soften.

'But why would you settle for this? This is a tragedy. You are a beautiful woman. What do you get from this kind of relationship?'

He thought her beautiful? *Don't think about that!*

'You mean besides a headache?' She pursed her lips. 'I've no idea.'

She typed *Report for Xavier: Suggested Repairs* across the top of the page.

'Believe me, I've thought about it—long and hard. The best I've come up with is that these men must bring out my maternal instincts, or something equally Freudian.'

He sat back, his brow furrowing. 'It is true that you are nurturing and kind. You were excellent with Serena yesterday.'

She couldn't have said why, but the compliment warmed her.

'I'm also a sucker for a hard luck story.'

She selected a bullet point list from the dropdown menu, and then glanced across to find him staring at her with a mystified expression.

She shrugged. 'I used to have this fantasy of being a—' She broke off with a laugh. 'Listen to me rabbit on.'

Talk less; work more.

'Rabbit?'

'It means talk too much.'

'No, this you do not do. You do not rabbit. Tell me this fantasy of yours.'

She gave up pretending to concentrate on the report. 'Fine—but only if this is tit for tat, quid pro quo, what's sauce for the goose is sauce for the gander and all that.'

She needed to find some common ground with this man. She was willing to try anything if it would help soften him.

A faint smile touched those sensual lips. 'All of these expressions I understand. You want to know what kind of woman I am drawn to, yes?'

'Yes.'

'Cruel women,' he said without hesitation.

It took an effort to keep her jaw from dropping. 'And what kind of satisfaction do *you* get from relationships with cruel women?'

'No satisfaction. Just disappointment.'

Heavens, what a pair they made. Not a *pair*, though, as in *couple*.

'Well, then…you're doubly safe, aren't you? You're not a no-hope loser and *I'm* most definitely not a cruel woman.'

'Very true.'

'But now I have to ask why? *Why* are you drawn to cruel women?'

He studied his hands for several long moments. 'I come from a very wealthy family. You know this, yes?'

Understanding dawned. 'All your life people have pandered to you—bowed and scraped, so to speak, because of your wealth and your position. So…you find cruel women refreshing?'

'I suppose that must be part of it. This lack of pandering, as you call it, always gives me the impression that they care nothing for my wealth or my social standing.'

'Oh, but—' She snapped her mouth shut.

His lips twisted. 'Yes. It is a false impression...a front. I learned that lesson early.'

Her research had revealed that Xavier was divorced, his marriage having only lasted two years. Had his wife been a cruel woman? Her heart beat hard, but she forced herself to recall the disdain in Xavier's eyes when she'd contemplated kissing him. She wanted him to be doubly—triply—sure that wouldn't happen again. *Ever.*

She lifted her chin. 'I know several very cruel women. Would you like me to introduce you to them during your stay here at the Gold Coast?'

He visibly shuddered. 'No, thank you.'

She refused to examine why his refusal made her breathe more easily.

'Now, tell me this fantasy of yours.'

'Oh, that.' She started to laugh. 'I've always had this secret yearning to be a wild woman—a *femme fatale* who attracts tall, dark and deliciously dangerous men.'

He raised one eyebrow. 'Dangerous?'

'Not *criminally* dangerous. But, you know—daredevils, pirates, rakes.'

'And what would you do with these...pirates?'

'Have wild, carefree flings and then toss them aside without a care once I was done with them.'

He spread his hands wide. 'Then why do you not do this?'

She sobered and tucked her hair back behind her ears. 'Because whenever I've tried in the past I've always found myself stuck in a corner with some soulful poet or oversensitive artist who's looking for a free bed, a free meal and a mummy substitute. I've had to face the hard truth, Xavier. I don't have a wild woman bone in my body.'

She shrugged.

'Besides, it's mean to treat people as if they're expendable and don't have feelings.' She rolled her eyes. 'I'm a good girl through and through, I'm afraid.'

'Why is this a bad thing?'

'You even have to ask?' He stared at her so blankly that she added, 'Have you ever dated a good girl?'

His brow furrowed. 'No.'

'And do you know why?'

'I…' He trailed off.

'Because they're boring! Because they remind you of your mother. And who wants to date their mother? No one. Except for…' She raised her eyebrows.

'Ah…' He nodded again. 'Except for these poets and artists of yours?'

'Exactly.'

He stared at her, and the intensity of his gaze made everything inside her clench.

'No more,' she said when he opened his mouth. 'I have to write this report.'

* * *

'Have you told him about us yet?' Tina demanded the next morning.

Wynne misjudged the first step of the stairs. She grabbed onto the bannister. 'There hasn't been time...or the opportunity.'

She didn't wait for a lecture, but set off straight up the stairs for the conference room. She needed to time her staffing policy revelation carefully.

Turning into the conference room, she came to the swift conclusion that the timing wasn't right this morning. If thunder had a face it would be Xavier's.

She bit back a sigh. This man, it appeared, lacked an inner cheer button. 'Good morning, Xavier.'

'Good morning, Wynne.'

At least he took the time to give her a salutation instead of barking questions and orders at her the moment she walked in. She set her laptop down and switched on the coffee percolator on the sideboard. Coffee was never a bad idea. A cheerful gurgle and the invigorating scent of coffee soon filled the air.

'Serena Gladstone phoned this morning to thank us for the huge bunch of flowers.' She sent him a smile over her shoulder. 'That was a lovely thing to do, Xavier. They're transferring her today to a hospital closer to where she lives. She's feeling much better and improving every day.'

'That is good to know.'

He looked a little embarrassed that his flower

gesture had been found out. She hid a smile as she made their coffees.

She slid a mug in front of him.

He cleared his throat. 'Now, perhaps you'll tell me about this?'

He sat at the head of the table and handed her a sheaf of papers. She slipped into the seat on his right and glanced at them. 'This is the report I wrote for you yesterday afternoon.'

'And you emailed to me late last night—*very* late.'

She sipped her coffee, surprised at his tight tone. 'Are you annoyed about that?'

Why should that annoy him?

She glanced down at her report, frowning. 'Is there something wrong with this?'

'What is wrong is that you work outrageous hours! You're up at the crack of dawn to do the breakfasts and then…and then you continue through all hours of the night writing reports.'

She hadn't had time to finish it before dinner had had to be started. She'd spent an hour after dinner finishing it. She'd then let it sit for a while before reading it over and deciding it was fit to send.

'What is *wrong*, Wynne Antonia Stephens—'

Whoa! He had that tone down pat. She found herself fighting the desire to fidget. As if she were guilty of some crime.

'—is that you spent what should be your leisure time writing a work report!'

'Oh…um…' She didn't know what to say.

His glare deepened. 'I do not expect you to work twenty-four hours a day seven days a week.'

'No, of course you don't.'

Was he worried she'd sue him for poor work-place practices?

'Going from owner-manager to manager is an… interesting transition.' Deep inside an ache started up. 'I mean, I used to be on call twenty-four-seven.' *When Aggie's Retreat had been hers.* 'And I believe that as your manager I need to be flexible in my hours. I mean, I took most of Tuesday afternoon off.'

'Off?' He stared at her in so much outrage his hair seemed to bristle with it. 'You were looking after Serena Gladstone!'

'But it wasn't actual *work*.'

'You were looking after a client's needs!'

She wished he'd stop yelling at her. She forced her chin up. 'You're paying me a very generous wage. I intend to earn it.'

His mouth firmed. 'You will not work all the hours of the week, Wynne. It leads to burnout. And burnout is an inefficient business practice.'

She only just prevented herself from clapping a hand to her brow and saying, *Silly me! Of course it is!*

She shuffled forward. 'Okay, how's this for a plan? During the busy periods I work long hours.

It's inevitable. This is the hotel business after all,' she added when he looked as if he'd argue.

'It is not how my five-star hotels are run.'

'Of course not—but this is a much smaller operation. It's a very different beast from one of your giant hotels.'

'And what do you get for working all these very long hours?'

'Your undying admiration?'

He didn't crack even the faintest of smiles. She recalled that moment on the stairs yesterday afternoon and decided it might be better not to joke with this man. He might take it the wrong way. He might misinterpret it as flirtation.

'What I get in return, Xavier, is a corresponding flexibility from you.'

'Explain.'

'I get to take that extra time worked in lieu. If I need an hour off for a doctor's appointment I'm free to take that hour. If I work fifteen hours one day I get to take the following afternoon off. That sort of thing. Obviously if you want me to keep a timesheet I will.'

Ugh.

'I am tempted to insist upon it—just so you are forced to acknowledge how many hours you work—but as I can see you loathe the idea I will let it drop for now.'

'Thank you.'

'Also, you will take this afternoon off in lieu of all the overtime you've worked this week.'

A free afternoon would be a godsend, but...

'How do you know how much overtime I've been working?'

Did his lips twitch upwards the tiniest fraction?

'Tina has a very high opinion of you.'

Ah... She couldn't work out if, in his eyes, that was a good thing or not.

'You are flexible with her hours because she is a single mother, yes?'

'Tina is a gem and I want to hold on to her.' Her mouth dried. 'I try to be flexible with all my staff. Within reason,' she added, because it seemed wise to add it even if it wasn't a hundred per cent true. 'I find that it earns me staff loyalty and goodwill.'

He glanced at his computer and pushed a couple of keys. 'Unfortunately that is not reflected in the efficiency rates of your housekeeping staff.'

'No, it wouldn't be.'

Boom. Boom. Boom. The blood pounded in her ears.

'But I would argue that those efficiency rates aren't as important in a small concern like Aggie's Retreat as they are in one of your big five-star hotels.' She bit her lip. 'I could write you a report.'

'That won't be necessary. It is not on my agenda for today.'

She had a reprieve? *Thank you, God!*

'And you will *not* write a report on your afternoon off. Is that clear?'

Whoa! Serious glare. 'Crystal.' She nodded, happy to move his thoughts away from possible staffing cuts and changes.

It was only a temporary reprieve, and in her mind she started writing a report anyway.

'So you will take the afternoon off and we'll work hard this morning, yes?'

She straightened. 'Yes. Thank you.'

'Now, to today's business. I am changing the name of the motel.'

Her heart gave a funny little clutch, but it was gone again in an instant. She nodded. 'That's not wholly unexpected.'

He stared at her as if he hadn't anticipated such easy acquiescence. She stared back steadily enough. Two years ago such news might have shattered her, but the last two years had shown her what really mattered. A motel name-change was nothing to watching her grandmother's slow decline. *That* was what raked ugly claws through her heart, shredding it until she almost wished she didn't have a heart left. What the darn motel happened to be called wasn't on the same scale.

She rested her hands on the table and sent him a smile meant to reassure him. 'What will you call it instead? I won't deny that it'll take some getting used to. I hope you have something colourful picked out.'

'Villa Lorenzo.'

His grandfather's name? She repeated it slowly. 'It has a nice ring to it.' She reached out and briefly clasped his hand. 'It's a lovely tribute.'

She refused to let her hand linger against the intriguing warmth of his. Releasing him, she pulled her laptop towards her and started making notes.

'I'll organise new stationery immediately, and the sign out at the front will need to be changed. I'll organise that too. Are you happy for me to use local businesses?'

She glanced up to find he'd pressed a thumb and forefinger to his eyes.

A headache? Or grief?

'Would you like me to get you some aspirin?'

He pulled his hand away. 'No. I'm fine. Thank you. And yes to using local businesses. It is usually...politic. I'd like the new sign fast-tracked if possible. I'm prepared to pay double the going rate to have that happen.'

She jotted that down. 'Would you like me to make some phone calls now?'

He glanced at his watch. 'If you can be done in fifteen minutes then, yes. We have an appointment and the car will be coming to collect us at nine-thirty.'

'I'll be ready,' she promised.

She tripped out without another word, saluting the Captain silently as she went past.

'We've come to the Golden Palace?'

Wynne peered out of the limousine's windows

as the car was ushered through the security gates of one of Surfers Paradise's most exclusive resorts. Today—unlike Tuesday—she'd taken such simple delight in the short limousine journey—exclaiming over the crystal wine decanter and glasses and luxuriating in the expanse of space—that Xavier wished the journey had been longer.

'I want you to see what the Golden Palace offers its clients.'

He was well aware of the resort's prestige. And he had hotels dotted about the globe that matched and in some instances exceeded the Golden Palace's luxury. He wanted Wynne to see it—to understand what he wanted to achieve with the Villa Lorenzo. That name, though, was only temporary. It would take many, many months before demolition could begin on the existing building and The Lorenzo could be erected in its place. In the meantime he refused to accept that any hotel of his would bear *that woman's* name a moment longer.

Wynne sat back and folded her arms. 'I already know what it offers. It has Italian marble bathrooms, gold-plated fixtures, a resort-style pool…and its own private access to the beach.'

He frowned at the stubborn jut of her jaw. The Golden Palace was a haven of calm, sophistication and good taste. 'You will take careful note of all we see here this morning,' he ordered, his voice sharp.

Her jaw lowered. 'Yes, of course.'

Why did he get the feeling her deference only went skin-deep?

He rolled his shoulders. Why should that bother him? He owned Aggie's Retreat—*Villa Lorenzo*. Where the motel was concerned, his word was now law.

The limousine drew to a halt and Wynne immediately slid out.

He bit back a sigh. 'Wynne, we have a driver to open the car doors.'

'Ah, but you also have a hotel manager, and I don't expect your staff to wait on me…*sir*.'

So his order had ruffled her feathers, had it? 'You will call me Xavier.' He made his voice short and tart.

'Yes, of course… Sir Xavier.'

But her lips twitched as she said it, and he found himself having to bite back a smile. The woman was irrepressible. And she had a finely honed sense of the ridiculous. She loved to laugh at herself…and at him. And he was starting to find that he didn't mind that so much.

But now to business.

'Mr Ramos, I'm Judith—one of the managers here at the Golden Palace. We're delighted to have you visit us. Mr Fontaine sends his express greetings and apologies. He's sorry he can't take you for the tour personally.'

Xavier introduced Wynne, and the two women shook hands.

Wynne pointed. 'Your scarf…is it Hermès?'

'Yes.'

When Xavier raised an eyebrow at her, she merely shrugged. 'Just taking note of everything, as you ordered. So far I've noted that Judith's scarf is worth more than my entire outfit.'

'Is there some point you're making?'

'None at all…' her eyes twinkled '…yet.'

The tour of the hotel took an hour.

Wynne did not display any of the delight that she had in the limousine—although both the public spaces and private rooms were exquisite. She made polite small talk with Judith, and asked intelligent questions, but beneath it all he sensed her silent disapproval. And the more he sensed it, the more Xavier could feel himself clenching up.

The tour ended with Judith settling them at a table shaded by a large umbrella on the sun-drenched terrace and ordering them refreshments.

'Please let me know if there's anything else I can help you with.'

With a nod she was gone, discretion itself. He wondered if Wynne could learn that same trick.

Surprisingly enough, he didn't doubt her ability to run an establishment like this. He had a feeling she could do that standing on her head. Wynne Antonia Stephens was a woman of many talents. He just doubted her ability to be quite so…*invisible*.

CHAPTER FIVE

Wynne gestured around the terrace, her nostrils flaring. '*This* is what you want to achieve at Villa Lorenzo?'

He refused to allow her disapproval to touch him. He intended to create a motel that would do Lorenzo proud—he would not be swayed from that purpose.

'*Objectively*, what do you think of the Golden Palace?'

'You want to know what I *noted*?'

'You are still angry with me for my request?'

'I'm not angry at *what* you asked of me—I'm angry at the *way* you asked it. It wasn't a request. It was a demand.'

He thrust out his jaw. 'I am not used to couching requests to my staff in a manner meant to pander to their sensibilities. My request was not unreasonable.'

But she wasn't listening to him. Her attention had been snagged by a little boy—a child no older than Luis—who was walking across the terrace, crying. Behind the glass of both the restaurant and the foyer staff watched, but nobody made a move to approach the child.

'Oh, for heaven's sake!'

Wynne leapt to her feet and raced across to the little boy.

Crouching down, she smiled at him. 'Hello, pumpkin, are you lost?'

He nodded in a woebegone way, hiccupping through his tears. Wynne reached out and wiped them away. Xavier glanced around. Why did none of the staff come out to help the child?

'My name is Wynne. Would you like to come and sit at the table over there with me and my friend until your mummy or daddy or your nanny come and find you?' She did a cute little excited shimmy. 'We have lemonade, and it's so yummy.'

And then the little boy was in her arms and she'd brought him back to the table and cuddled him on her lap, letting him sip lemonade from her glass until he was smiling again and all traces of his tears were gone.

Yearning suddenly gripped him. He missed Luis. It was time Luis and Paula finished their sightseeing in Sydney and came to the Gold Coast. Luis had been too quiet and too withdrawn lately. He needed to get to the bottom of it.

The little boy stayed with them for ten minutes before his nanny was found. She'd been on the phone to her boyfriend. Apparently she'd thought he was asleep. *Dios!* He knew the staff would report the incident *discreetly* to the boy's parents.

Wynne watched the little boy disappear with a

martial light in her eyes. She swung back to Xavier. 'I couldn't just ignore him.'

She said it as if she expected his displeasure. *Dios.*

'I am glad you did not.' If Luis ever found himself in such a situation he hoped someone like Wynne would take him under their wing.

She sat back and folded her arms. 'So…you want to know what I *noted* about this pantheon of luxury?'

It was all he could do not to wince at her scorn.

'Other than the fact that—as I said before—the staff's scarves are worth more than my entire outfit, did you notice that all the staff here are physically very beautiful?'

He hadn't. Though he was starting to find that when Wynne was around everything else seemed to fade into the background.

'Why should that bother you?'

'Because plain people and physically imperfect people make just as good employees as beautiful people.'

He chose his words carefully. 'A place like the Golden Palace provides its clients with a fantasy. Here, beauty is the ideal.'

Her brow furrowed. 'And that doesn't bother you?'

She made him sound shallow!

He fought back a scowl. 'It is a fact of life. It is admittedly perhaps a little unfair…'

'Oh, you *think*?'

He sent her the glare that usually had his employees trembling and backtracking. She lowered her gaze—eventually—but if there was any trembling it was due only to her frustration.

'Tell me what else you observed.'

'I saw that woman—a guest—in the dining area, making a scene because the waitress had served her a cappuccino rather than a latte.' She rolled her eyes. 'She threw a temper tantrum *over a coffee*.'

'The staff should not make such mistakes.'

'The staff are human—not robots. If I were the manager here I wouldn't let anyone speak to my staff that way.'

He stared at her, intrigued in spite of himself. 'You do not subscribe to the motto "the customer is always right"?'

'The customer *isn't* always right. I do my best to accommodate our guests' wishes and requests at Aggie's Retreat, but I demand respect in return. There's absolutely no need to speak to anyone the way that woman spoke to the staff.'

He'd noticed the woman—she'd reminded him of Camilla. Secretly he agreed with Wynne, but...

'Difficult guests are part of the business.'

She remained silent.

He folded his arms, tamping down on the laugh rising in his chest. 'Why do I get the feeling that in the past you might have told some guests that their business was no longer welcome at Aggie's Retreat?'

Her gaze abruptly dropped to her glass of lemonade. She stirred it with her straw.

'It works both ways, though. Did you see how supercilious that darn concierge was when a guest was asking directions to a restaurant?'

He frowned. 'I did not.'

'He deliberately acted superior to make the man nervous. It was uncalled for.'

If that was the truth, then she had his wholehearted agreement.

'That man was obviously not wealthy. I mean not on the scale that many of the clientele here will be. He's probably scrimped and saved for an entire year to give himself and his wife this amazing treat…and yet does he get treated with equal deference as the coffee tantrum-thrower? Is his money not as good? The unfairness of it makes me so mad!'

Her eyes flashed green fire and her hair crackled about her face and for a moment Xavier couldn't speak for the unholy thirst that gripped him. Today, if she stood a step above him and gazed at his lips with the same hunger as she had yesterday, he wouldn't hesitate to wrap an arm about her waist and drag her mouth to his to slake the heat rising through him.

He didn't know if that made him a fool for not taking the chance yesterday, or a fool for wanting that same opportunity today.

She slashed a hand through the air. 'I'm sorry. I feel passionately about this.'

'So I can see.'

'One thing we *have* achieved at Aggie's Retreat—'

Those glorious eyes sparked and he had the distinct impression she called it Aggie's Retreat rather than Villa Lorenzo on purpose.

'—is that we do our utmost to make *everyone* feel equally welcome.'

He recalled the afternoon tea that she had arranged for him—the one he hadn't partaken of. It had been a nice gesture.

'Seriously, Xavier, is *this*—' she gestured to the hotel '—the kind of homage you want to pay Lorenzo?'

'This is the best the Gold Coast has to offer.' A fist tightened about his chest. 'My grandfather deserves the best!'

'It's the most *luxurious*. It's the most *expensive*. It doesn't automatically follow that it's the best.' She blew out a breath, sagging back in her chair. 'I thought you said we were on the same page where the motel was concerned?'

Nausea churned through him. He held himself rigid. 'You said you wanted the motel to succeed. As do I. I never once said that I shared your vision for Aggie's Retreat.'

Hurt flashed in those eyes before her gaze was abruptly removed from his. He wanted to yell at her, tell her that she'd overstepped the bounds, but she hadn't.

He swore in Spanish. 'For pity's sake, Wynne. Not by any standards does Aggie's Retreat fit the image of a modern, convenient business hotel.

'If by "modern" you mean impersonal—'

He held up his hand and she snapped her mouth shut while he searched his phone for the review he'd bookmarked earlier. 'I have a review here that lists in detail all the flaws of your beloved Aggie's Retreat.'

She folded her arms and lifted her chin.

'"One: the motel is not on the hotel mini-bus route from the airport, making it difficult to get to."'

'We're a *motor* inn, Xavier. The majority of our guests drive their own cars.'

'"Two: Surfers Paradise is one of the most beautiful strips of beach in the world, but the motel has neither beach nor canal views."'

'Both are easily accessed.'

'"The oddly designed building was built in the nineteen-eighties, though it looks nothing like a modern motel…"'

'I'd take that as a compliment rather than a criticism.'

He continued to read. '"There is no business centre, gym or swimming pool…"'

'We have a conference room.'

'Which is poorly equipped,' he felt compelled to point out.

'*And* free WiFi.'

Xavier read on. '"The rooms are advertised as having balconies, but as my room faced a busy road its balcony was a glassed-in sunroom, which made it unsuitable for an after-dinner cigar."'

Unexpectedly Wynne's face cleared, but when she didn't proceed to give him a lecture about the sins of smoking, he pressed on.

'"The faux Victorian furniture is twee. It must also be noted that the motel has an extremely limited meal service."'

He switched off his phone and dropped it to the table. 'The motel is a mess!'

She seized her own phone. 'Shame on you. I know exactly which review you just referred to. It's Mick Bowen's, and he goes on to say that despite all those failings he wouldn't stay anywhere else when he's visiting this part of the world. He praises the made-to-order breakfasts, the firm beds and deep pillows. He appreciates the size of the rooms and the cleanliness of the bathrooms.' She fixed him with a glare that was half-triumph half-annoyance. 'You'll have noticed that he says *"the hospitality is exceptional."*'

Xavier tried to smother a scowl.

She flung both arms out wide. 'Have you ever read a better review in your life?'

'It doesn't change the fact that the motel needs work!'

'Work that you can afford to do without destroying the tenor of the place or its…*spirit*. That review makes it clear what the clientele value. Shouldn't you be capitalising on the motel's strengths?'

'I do five-star hotels—not three-star motor inns!'

'Well, maybe it's time you started—because the one thing the Gold Coast doesn't need is another luxury hotel!'

They both seemed to realise at the same time that they were half out of their chairs and yelling.

They both sat back.

Wynne straightened her blouse. 'You're a businessman, Xavier. It doesn't matter how much money you throw at the place, you're never going to manage beach views. As for a resort-style pool—there's just not enough room. So why on earth would the coffee tantrum-throwing crowd ever choose Villa Lorenzo over the Golden Palace?'

'If I build up, the hotel will have beach views one side and canal views on the other. If I build up I can put a resort pool on the roof.'

She stilled as if he'd slid a knife in between her ribs—as if by remaining still it would mitigate the pain. His heart started to pound. It was *his* hotel!

Finally she swallowed. 'You mean demolish the existing building?'

He kept his chin raised, but his heart started to ache—which made no sense at all. 'That's exactly what I mean.'

'To build something on the same scale as this?'

He thrust his jaw out. 'Better than this.'

'You think Lorenzo would choose marble bathrooms and gold taps over warmth and kindness?'

'It doesn't have to be either or!'

'Really? Well, let me tell you something for nothing, Xavier. The staff here wouldn't intrude on a client who had their *Do Not Disturb* sign up. They wouldn't dare, for fear of looking *unprofessional*. And apparently their mission statement doesn't run to consoling a child. They're too afraid to give a crying four-year-old a cuddle because—heaven forbid—it might upset his parents!'

Her words speared into the centre of him. She hadn't cared what anyone thought when she'd pulled that little boy onto her lap. She'd just wanted to comfort him. He admired her for it.

She pointed a finger at him and he couldn't help but notice how it trembled.

'That's not a world I want to live in. And I wouldn't have thought it was one you wanted to live in either.'

He pushed his chair back and shot to his feet. She didn't know it, but she'd just accused him of being like his grandmother—entitled, selfish... cold. A part of him couldn't help wondering if she was right. A part of him couldn't help wondering if that was the reason Luis had become so guarded around him.

He made his voice as frosty as he could. 'You're straying perilously close to the personal, Wynne. It's time we returned to the motel.'

* * *

Wynne marched down the nursing home's corridor, hands clenched and mind racing. She *so* had to work on her deference skills. But...

He wanted to build a ludicrous palace to offer up on the altar of indulgence and extravagance! What was a body *supposed* to do? She and her staff would once again be told they weren't good enough, that they didn't measure up, and they'd all be out on their ears. It was enough to make her scream!

She'd been told she wasn't *good enough* for Duncan's world because she didn't wear designer clothes and apparently her robust social conscience was unfashionable—*'So last week, darling!'* The fact that she'd loved him hadn't counted for anything. He'd treated her like rubbish that needed disposing of—had mentally assigned her to the trash when he'd got what he'd wanted. That casual cruelty had turned her life upside down.

Libby and the others from the Down Syndrome shelter weren't considered *good enough* because they'd been born a bit different. Her teeth ground together. They had as much right as anyone to a place in the world.

As for April and Justin... Sure, they'd made mistakes—mistakes that had cost them dearly—but everyone was entitled to a second chance.

They were all *good enough* and she wouldn't let anyone tell them differently! She wouldn't let anyone break them the way Duncan had almost broken her.

She came to an abrupt halt.

Could she change Xavier's mind?

The Golden Palace provided excellence in standards and service, but where was the brotherly love and the milk of human kindness? It'd been sacrificed for efficiency and opulence. She'd forced Xavier to see the impersonality and sterility hidden behind all that luxury…and the fact that the Golden Palace's benevolence only extended to the chosen few. He hadn't liked what he saw—hadn't approved of it. Surely it wasn't something he wanted to imitate or support?

It might yet be possible to change his mind.

Yeah, right, and pigs might fly.

She set off once more for her grandmother's room. She refused to surrender just yet. Xavier might think a luxurious monolith was a fitting tribute to Lorenzo, but maybe she could get him to see that something more…*human* would better commemorate Lorenzo's memory.

Or pigs might fly.

She bit back a sigh and entered her grandmother's room. She *so* had to work on her negotiation skills.

Aggie looked up. 'Do I know you, dear?'

'Hello, Nanna, it's Wynne'

'Wynne?'

'Your granddaughter.

'I have a granddaughter?'

'You do.'

It was the same ritual every visit. It no longer caught at her heart the way it had used to. Which just went to show that a body could get used to just about anything.

Aggie sat in a plush recliner. Wynne took the visitor's chair next to it and nodded towards the hot pink gerbera daisies sitting on the bedside table. 'They're pretty.'

'One of the nurses brings them in every week. At least she *says* she's a nurse, but I know that she's not.' She leaned forward in a confidential manner. 'She's really my daughter.'

'Coral?'

'Is that my daughter's name? Well, yes, of course it is. Yes—Coral brings them every week. She's going to take me home soon.'

Wynne had a standing order with a local florist, and she knew that Aggie would never be coming home, but she didn't have the heart to tell her either of those things. Aggie received the very best of care here, and she had an opportunity to mix with the other folk in the nursing home too, as well as to attend the occasional outing. And yet she'd never been able to reconcile herself to being there.

'Coral is in France, Nanna.' She lifted the latest postcard propped up against the vase. 'See? She sends her love.'

'She'll be back to take me home soon.'

Wynne pulled a bag of sweets from her purse. 'I brought you a present.'

Aggie's face lit up. She reached into the bag and pulled out several jelly babies, the creases around her eyes deepening in pleasure as she munched on the sweets. Wynne savoured the moment. Seeing her grandmother enjoy herself had become the exception rather than the rule. Wynne couldn't get used to that. The memory loss and the confusion she could harden herself to, but not Aggie's lack of joy…her misery and fury.

More and more she'd gone from someone determined to wring every drop of pleasure from each day to an angry, resentful stranger.

'Nanna, do you remember a man from Spain called Lorenzo?'

Aggie stilled, and just for a moment Wynne thought the shock of hearing the name might bring a long-buried memory to the fore…that for a few brief moments a lucid Aggie would emerge. It did still happen on occasions.

This wasn't one of those occasions.

'The nurses are trying to kill me.'

Aggie's face darkened and Wynne bit back a sigh. 'But they bring you flowers.'

'They want my money.'

Wynne shook her head. 'You don't have any money, Nanna.'

'But I need money to buy my lunch. What will I do if I can't buy my lunch?'

'That's all been taken care of. You don't have to worry about money any more.'

The faded blue eyes grew cloudy with confusion. 'You're my granddaughter?'

'That's right. I'm Wynne.'

Aggie's chin wobbled. 'Will you take me home?'

A lump formed in her throat and her eyes stung. 'This *is* your home now. Don't you remember?'

Aggie's lips twisted and her eyes flashed. 'You're my granddaughter, but you won't take me home? You must be a bad granddaughter.' Her voice rose. 'You must be a wicked girl!'

A handful of jelly babies flew across to pelt Wynne's cheek and neck.

'You're trying to kill me too!'

Two nurses rushed into the room. One planted a placating hand on Aggie's arm. 'Now, now, Ms Stephens, we don't want you getting too excited. Remember what the doctor said?'

Aggie let her second handful of jelly baby ammunition drop to her lap. 'Have I been ill?'

'That's right.'

The other nurse gently but inexorably led Wynne from the room. 'It's probably best if your grandmother rests now.'

Wynne couldn't stop from glancing back over her shoulder at Aggie. Her heart clutched at how small and frail and scared her grandmother looked.

'I promise she's getting the very best of care.'

'I know,' Wynne managed through the lump in her throat. 'And I'm truly grateful.'

She held off the tears until she was inside her car, where they wouldn't inconvenience anyone.

Wynne didn't return to the hotel until nearly four o'clock.

'I said I want that picture removed *now*!'

Wynne stumbled to a halt in the foyer doorway as Xavier's lethal tones reached her. *Dear God!* Xavier loomed across the check-in desk over a white-faced but defiant Tina. Neither one of them had seen her.

She closed her eyes and pulled in a breath.

Right. Bright. Breezy. Deferential. Smile!

'Good afternoon, Xavier… Tina.'

She breezed in as if she didn't have a care in the world…picking up the mail and flicking through it as she moved behind the counter…as if it *hadn't* shaken her to find Xavier castigating her staff in tones that would have made her want to shrivel up inside if they'd been directed at her.

'Xavier, I couldn't help overhearing you just now. When, precisely, did you make your request to have Aggie's portrait taken down?'

His eyes shot white-hot sparks across the distance between them. 'You're supposed to be out. Away. Enjoying your free afternoon.' Each word was bitten out.

'I had a lovely time, thank you.'

How on earth was she going to fix this? Difficult

customers were one thing. A difficult boss was an altogether scarier proposition. She'd known her observations at the Golden Palace earlier had raised his hackles. She'd expected him to take it out on *her*, though, not on anyone else.

She set the mail down. 'Tina, when did Mr Ramos request that Aggie's portrait be taken down?'

'Just after you left. At around twelve-thirty.'

Tina's words emerged short and clipped, and it was all Wynne could do not to wince.

Xavier looked at his watch. 'It is now after four. I refuse to countenance such blatant insubordination.'

'So my free afternoon was granted to me entirely altruistically, was it?'

He scowled at her. She shrugged. It was better than him scowling at Tina. Tina didn't get paid enough to put up with that sort of nonsense.

'Tina, would you be an absolute love and put the kettle on? I expect the boys will be trooping in shortly for a glass of milk and a cookie, and I'd kill for a cup of tea.'

Tina left and Wynne turned back to Xavier. 'On Thursdays the maintenance man works until midday. If you'd made your request prior to that, the picture would've been taken down today.' She held up a hand when he looked as if he were about to speak. 'It's not just that it *isn't* Tina's job to clamber up a ladder to remove a picture—it's an Occupational Health and Safety issue.'

He slammed his hands on his hips. 'Why did she not explain this to me herself?'

'Did you give her the chance?'

The flare of his nostrils told its own story. No, he hadn't. Instead he'd flown off the handle, interpreting Tina's actions as a deliberate act of rebellion.

'So yelling at Tina as if she were an…an utter incompetent is how you saw fit to deal with this?'

His lethal gaze swung back to her. '*You* will take care not to speak to *me* as if *I* am an utter incompetent!'

He stabbed a finger at her and something inside her snapped. 'As soon as you stop *acting* like an utter incompetent *and* a bully, I'll stop treating you like one! Your behaviour as I walked into the foyer this afternoon wasn't just appalling but totally unacceptable! It bordered on workplace bullying! Back in Spain you might be a total autocrat, but here you *will* learn to treat your staff with the respect they deserve. They're not peasants that you can stomp beneath your feet, or minions to be crushed to your will or…or… They're just good people, doing their best to lead good lives!'

His face turned black. 'You're—'

'No!' She cut him off. He *couldn't* fire her. She grasped for a straw and found one. 'What kind of example is that to set for your son?'

He blinked, and some of the fire drained from his eyes.

She gulped.

Their gazes clashed and locked. The very air between them seemed to simmer. For a moment he appeared darker, taller, stronger, and something inside her yearned towards him.

And then the drawing room door was flung open and both Blake and Heath came hurling out. 'Wynne, is Luis here yet? We need him to play cricket!'

'I'm afraid not.' She glanced at Xavier. 'Do we know when Luis is arriving?'

He stared at each of them in turn, his gaze hooded. 'Tomorrow.'

Both boys cheered and Wynne ushered them back into the drawing room. She took a deep breath before turning and facing Xavier once more.

He rubbed his nape. 'They are nice boys.'

'Yes.'

His dark eyes throbbed into hers. 'I overreacted with Tina.'

'Yes.' She kept herself to single syllables, not trusting herself with anything more.

'You are…cross with me, yes?'

'Furious.' Oops, that was three syllables.

'How can I temper this fury?'

She folded her arms. 'You can start by apologising to Tina.'

He spun on his heel and entered the drawing room. 'Tina?'

Wynne glanced over his shoulder to see Tina turn to him warily.

'I am very sorry for the way I spoke to you earlier. It was out of line. I promise it won't happen again.'

Tina swallowed, nodded, shrugged. 'No problem. It's all good.'

Xavier came back into the foyer and Wynne ducked behind the counter. She needed to keep it between herself and Xavier. It made her feel…*safer*. Especially now his anger was spent.

She straightened a pen, the phone, the computer. Xavier moved to lean on the counter, those watchful eyes making her want to fidget even more.

'How is your fury now?'

'Starting to diminish.'

'Not gone completely?'

She shook her head.

'I should apologise to you too, Wynne. Today has not gone as I'd planned or hoped.'

That much was evident.

'And then I came down here and saw Aggie's picture still on the wall, after I'd asked Tina to have it removed, and…' He glanced up at the portrait, his eyes stormy. 'It felt like she was laughing at me in the same way she must've laughed at Lorenzo.'

The lines about his mouth deepened. His grief was so deep and so raw. She wished she could help allay it.

'So you lost your temper?'

He dragged a hand down his face.

'And then you jumped to unfounded conclusions. Xavier, I know you're grieving for your grandfather, and I'm truly sorry for that, but you can't talk to the staff the way you just spoke to Tina. It's not fair. Please stop treating us like your enemies. We're not plotting behind your back. Do you truly begrudge us the fond memories we have of Aggie's Retreat? They won't prevent us from developing fond memories of Villa Lorenzo too.'

Though heaven only knew how long the Villa Lorenzo would remain before he tore it all down.

'Things change…time moves on…' Lives were upended and hearts broken. 'We're all aware of that.'

Beneath his tan he'd paled, and she knew she'd made her point.

'So to a couple of practical issues,' she pressed on. 'The maintenance man won't be back till Saturday. I can have Aggie's portrait removed then. My job description doesn't involve climbing ladders either, but if you decide yours does then a ladder is kept locked in the storeroom cupboard beneath the second staircase. The key is in the drawer here. Also, you need to know that it's been a long time since we've painted these walls. There's going to be a noticeable rectangle on the wall once that picture comes down. All the paint around it will have faded. Have you thought what you might like to put up there instead? Do you have a picture of Lorenzo we could put up in its place?'

She sounded so reasonable.
She *acted* so reasonable!

Xavier pressed his fingers to his eyes, leaning heavily against the counter. He should have waited twelve months before coming out here. He should have waited for the worst of his grief to pass.

The moment his grandfather had told him the story about this motel, though, revealing his heartbreak, Xavier had wanted to act. At once. He'd hoped it would make him feel better. It hadn't. It had been nothing more than a flimsy excuse to hide from his grief.

Still, none of that meant he had to put up with Aggie's portrait on the wall for another day!

Reaching across the counter, he removed the storeroom key from the drawer Wynne had indicated.

CHAPTER SIX

XAVIER WAS AWARE of Wynne's silent stare when he returned with the ladder. He wanted triumph to flood him as he lifted the portrait off the wall. Instead all he felt was a prickling awareness that lifted the small hairs at his nape as she watched him with those unflinching jade eyes.

He stepped off the last rung and rested the portrait against the stool. 'I would like you to throw that in the skip.' A couple of beats passed and he forced himself to add a belated, 'Please.'

'Besides the fact that we don't have a skip, I'm afraid this portrait is my personal property. But never fear—I'll remove it from the premises *pronto*.'

She opened her mouth as if to add something, but then glanced past him, a smile transforming her face. That smile held him still while his heart dashed itself against his ribs. Her smiles were so wide and genuine. And she was so free and easy with them!

Swallowing, he turned to see who the lucky recipient was and found a woman dressed in a smart navy suit striding towards the counter.

'Believe me, Wynne, this place is a sight for sore eyes today.'

'I shudder to think what time you hit the road

this morning, Carmen, but you've made excellent time. Keep this up and you might even get to spend the weekend with that gorgeous grandson of yours.'

'That's the plan.'

When Wynne handed the woman a room key with a cheery, 'Your usual room is free,' he assumed that this Carmen must be a regular guest.

'I'm cooking tonight, if you're interested.'

'Thanks, Wynne, but I have a hankering for Thai.' She pointed. 'What's the deal with Aggie's picture?'

'Oh! Carmen—this is Xavier Ramos. He's the motel's new owner and we're getting a name-change in honour of his grandfather—Villa Lorenzo. So we're going to pop up a portrait of Lorenzo. We're in for a bit of refurbishment too. Exciting times!'

Not an ounce of resentment threaded through her voice or flitted across her face.

Carmen turned alarmed eyes on him. 'I hope you don't mean to change the place too much. This is my home away from home.'

'I hope it will continue to remain so,' he returned smoothly.

But her suit was off-the-rack and both her hand-bag and shoes showed signs of wear. This Carmen would not be able to afford to stay in the Lorenzo, once it was completed. He pushed his shoulders back. There were many other three-star motor inns in the Gold Coast. In the meantime she would be very welcome at Villa Lorenzo.

Her eyes narrowed and she swung back to Wynne. 'He's going to get rid of the Old English Victorian manor feel of the place, isn't he?'

'Nothing is decided yet. So far we've just been tossing around a few ideas. But, dear Lord, Carmen—all of the carpet needs to come up, new window dressings wouldn't go astray, and even *you* have to admit that all the wood panelling is a bit…naff.'

'Well…perhaps a little.'

Xavier watched in astonishment as Wynne turned Carmen's ambivalence slowly on its head.

'Xavier, I just had a thought!' Wynne shimmied on the spot. 'Given your grandfather's heritage, and yours, what if we went with a Spanish theme for the motel? That'd be a lovely homage to your grandfather. We could keep the individuality of the rooms still, but tie them together with the Spanish theme.'

It would be the perfect revenge on Aggie. Did she not realise that?

Of course she did. But he was starting to see that she really didn't care about Aggie and Lorenzo's history. It left him feeling…flat.

'I've always wanted to go to Spain,' Carmen breathed.

He'd lay money on the fact that Wynne had known that too. His motel manager was crafty and astute. And kind and generous and warm-hearted.

And far from timid—which was what she'd accused Lorenzo of being. What would *she* do if she ever fell in love? What lengths would *she* go to in order to win her lover's heart?

What lengths would he himself go?

He shook himself free of that thought. He had no intention of falling in love. *Ever.* He was never giving a woman the kind of power that Aggie had wielded over Lorenzo. That kind of power brought a man to his knees and broke him.

He wasn't even giving a woman the power he'd given to Camilla. He had a son and heir. Marriage no longer held any allure for him.

'Before you go, Carmen, that red Corvette is up for sale.' Wynne retrieved an envelope from beneath the counter. 'Here are the details.'

Her grin made his chest catch.

'So now you have an enviable choice in front of you—a trip to Spain next year or a little red Corvette.'

'You're a wicked woman, Wynne!' Carmen took the envelope. 'Speaking of wicked women—how's Aggie?'

A shadow passed across Wynne's face. 'Same old, same old.'

'I bought her a present. Send my love the next time you see her.'

'That's kind of you, Carmen. I will.'

'Why did you do that?' he asked when Carmen had disappeared.

She glanced at him from the corner of her eyes.

'Do what? You might want to give me a little more to go on.'

He shifted his weight. 'Suggest the Spanish theme?'

'I thought you'd like it. I thought Lorenzo would like it. I mean, I know you're talking about building some outrageous skyscraper, but that's going to take time. In the meantime…' She trailed off with a shrug.

'Why should you care what Lorenzo would like?'

She folded her arms, turning and resting one hip against the counter. The portrait of Aggie hid most of her legs. Aggie smirked, as if she knew how much that irked him.

'I don't know how honest I should be here, Xavier.'

'I would like you to be fully honest. I assure you that this conversation will have no bearing on our working relationship. This is outside of that. I will not dismiss you for anything you say now.'

'Okay.' She pulled in a breath. 'The fact that your grandfather mentioned Aggie on his deathbed suggests to me that she had long been on his mind. It also leads me to think that he wasn't a happy man.' A frown darkened her eyes. She spoke slowly as if choosing her words with care. 'That he didn't lead a joyful life.'

An ache ballooned inside Xavier's chest. It was all he could do to keep breathing. Nobody could have managed joy when married to Xavier's grandmother. She hadn't been able to stand hearing people laugh, or endure seeing them have fun. She'd made Lorenzo miserable. How Lorenzo had resisted shrivelling up into a hard and bitter man was beyond him.

'It makes me think his marriage was not very happy.' Her gaze sharpened and her lips twisted. 'No doubt that was Aggie's fault as well.'

Just for a moment he saw Lorenzo—and himself—through her eyes, and he didn't like what he saw.

'Your grandfather created a great financial empire. He must've been very driven. But it seems to me that despite his wife and his three sons, and all his career success, he wasn't a happy man. My grandmother's life, in comparison, was very modest—and yet she lived her life with joy.'

His hands clenched. What right did Aggie have to that joy when she'd robbed his grandfather's life of happiness and peace?

'But if making over this motel in the style of your grandfather's heritage helps to heal that wound somehow, then I'm all for it. And, despite what you think, Aggie would be all for it too.'

'I want to meet her.'

Startled eyes met his. 'Aggie?'

He nodded.

She shook her head. 'Not a chance.'

'But—'

'Do you *really* think I'm going to give you a chance to speak to her in the same fashion you just have to me and Tina? You're a smarter man than that, Xavier.'

He'd just have to go behind her back, then. He had every intention of keeping his promise to Lorenzo.

She picked up Aggie's portrait and sent him a sweet smile. 'Now, if you'll excuse me, I believe this is my afternoon off.'

Xavier had gone to his room and tried to immerse himself in the endless emails that needed attention, but a *thwack-thwack* drifted in through his open balcony doors from the direction of Wynne's cottage.

He sat back. The land next door would be crucial to his plans. He'd give her a good price for it—an outrageous price if need be.

Thwack-thwack.

He rose. There was no time like the present to push for a deal.

The moment he entered Wynne's property through the side gate in the fence the reason behind the *thwack-thwack* became evident. She had her back to him and was wielding a paddle bat like an axe as she played a solitary game of… He wasn't sure what it was called in Australia—swing ball, totem tennis? Her every muscle bunched as she beat the blazes out of the ball. She looked as if she was fighting the world.

He raked a hand back through his hair. *Dios!* Had *he* done that to her?

She didn't know that he was there. He could turn around and creep away.

Another paddle bat lay on the grass nearby. He stared at it, and then with a smothered imprecation he seized it. In one smooth motion he'd joined the game.

Wynne didn't say anything, but she didn't break stride either. They played in silence for a while, and his chest clenched up tight at the set of her face.

'Is this because of me?' he asked finally. 'Your... anger? Is it because of how I behaved earlier?'

She missed a shot. 'No!'

Her genuine shock eased something inside him. He *never* wanted to be responsible for the desolation that stretched through her eyes, making her mouth thin and vulnerable.

She hit her next shot with extra venom and it was all he could do to return it.

'It's an old issue, Xavier. And there's nothing to be done. But sometimes playing an aggressive game of tether tennis helps.'

An old issue? A man?

A hard fist clenched in his chest. Had one of her no-hopers broken her heart? Was he still on the scene, causing her grief? If she confided in him, he would take care of the matter. With speed and ruthlessness. Wynne deserved better than a man who...who *used* her.

She was right—she wasn't a wild woman. Wild women were selfish, pleasure-seeking...reckless.

Wild women didn't care how their behaviour affected others. That wasn't Wynne. She held the hands of sick and frightened young women. She cuddled crying children.

The memory of her with that child on her lap…

Dios! He only just missed being hit by the ball as it whizzed past his nose. He half expected her to laugh and throw him some challenge. Laughter, however, did not light her eyes. He had a feeling she hadn't even noticed his missed shot.

She suddenly seemed to grow aware of his scrutiny. She served the ball to him again. 'You must've loved Lorenzo a great deal.'

Yearning stretched through her eyes, and he didn't know what she yearned for. He nodded, choosing to focus on answering the question before he became lost in that deep green. 'I did.'

'Tell me about him. Why did you love him so well?'

So he did. He told her about the holidays and weekends that he'd spent with Lorenzo. They'd been the one bright point in his otherwise lonely childhood. He related incidents he hadn't thought about in years.

She laughed when he described his and Lorenzo's botched attempt at topiary. His grandmother, unfortunately, hadn't seen the humour in the misshapen bushes and hedges on their rather grand estate in the hills of Malaga. But then his grandmother had been the antithesis of Lorenzo, and intent on eradicating anything she'd deemed as inappropriate, noisy or in bad taste. Apparently any form of fun had been in bad taste. Whenever she'd been around Lorenzo's laughter had fallen silent. The injustice of that still burned in Xavier's soul.

He told Wynne how Lorenzo had taken him exploring in the older part of town, with its winding cobbled alleys, where they'd eat paella from street vendors and talk and talk and talk.

He and Lorenzo had created their own little world, where laughter, curiosity and freedom had reigned supreme—so different from the real world they'd belonged to. A world defined by duty and status and the appearance of respectability. They'd found comfort and camaraderie in each other. When they'd returned to that real world they had both reverted to being silent loners.

For a moment Xavier missed his grandfather so much it was all he could do to keep his voice even, but as he talked his grandfather came alive for him again. And as he talked the tension in Wynne's shoulders gradually eased, the shadows in her eyes retreated, and the tight lines about her lips softened.

He didn't want to notice her lips—they sent his temperature soaring—but to know he'd helped to lighten her load in some small way made him feel... He pushed his shoulders back. It made him feel like a million dollars! He wished he could bottle the feeling so he could draw on it the next time she challenged him or took him to task.

Eventually Wynne lowered her bat. Her green eyes darkened. 'Thank you.'

He tried to shrug. 'I did nothing.'

She shook her head, the ghost of a smile playing across her lips. 'That's not true and you know it.'

And then, as if on impulse, she leaned forward and pressed a kiss to his cheek. The scent of jasmine and warm woman engulfed him. He clenched his hands to stop himself gathering her in and kissing her properly.

Images rose in his mind and hunger roared through him like a wind in his ears, deafening him, making him hyper-aware of the pulse pounding in his blood and the shine on Wynne's lips. She'd taken a step away from him, but paused now as if caught by the expression on his face. The green in her eyes flashed and sparked and he knew she felt it too.

For a moment he thought she might lean forward and press her lips to his. He held his breath…

With a tiny shake of her head, she stepped back. 'I…uh… Would you like a drink?'

When he nodded, she wiped her hands down the sides of her trousers—a nervous gesture that sent masculine satisfaction flooding through him. He couldn't recall wanting a woman with this kind of primitive hunger in… He couldn't remember how long! And she wanted him too. He could see it in the glitter of her eyes, the heightened colour at her cheekbones.

He lifted his chin. What was to stop them from

indulging in that passion? From giving each other pleasure?

'Right.' Her voice emerged on a breathless huff and she waved to her outdoor table setting. 'Why don't you take a seat?'

She fled inside. He sat, his heart pounding.

She returned a short time later with a jug of home-made lemonade. Ice clinked against its sides as she poured it into glasses, her hands not quite steady.

He surveyed her over the rim of his glass. She might call herself a good girl, but that didn't mean she'd necessarily view every romantic encounter as if it would lead to love and commitment.

Heat coiled in the pit of his belly. He would find out her position on that first. And then…

Fire licked along his nerve-endings. It had been too long since he'd felt this alive.

The expression on Xavier's face made Wynne's pulse do a Mexican Wave. She held on to her glass for grim life.

Dear God. It had been foolish to kiss Xavier—even innocently on the cheek.

Innocent? Raucous laughter sounded in her head. *Puhlease! You just wanted to feel the strength of him beneath your fingertips as you leant against him. You wanted to breathe him in.*

Oh, but he smelled so *good*! Breathing him in just made her feel…*easier*, somehow. As for the rest of him…

His hard strength through the thin cotton of his shirt had seared her palms. They tingled still. It had been the height of foolishness to touch him like that. Even now her pulse refused to settle.

Stop it! Think of something to say.

'Are you close to your parents, Xavier?'

Dear God, find something to talk about that's not personal!

'I respect them.'

That pulled her out of her fog. Talk about damned with faint praise.

He glanced at her from beneath dark winged brows. 'It is fair to say that my parents are naturally reserved and very...proper.'

Cold.

'They ensured that I attended the very best boarding schools.'

They'd sent him to *boarding school*? She suppressed a shudder. 'How old were you when you first attended?'

'Five.'

Dear God.

'My university was also of the highest standard. I have been granted the very best of opportunities.'

'But...you don't speak of your parents with the same warmth that you do of Lorenzo.'

'Lorenzo and I were...how do you say it? Kindred spirits.'

She suddenly saw that Lorenzo had been the one bright light in what must have been a very lonely childhood. No wonder Xavier's grief ran so deep.

'I'm utterly convinced that I'd have liked Lorenzo.'

'He'd have liked you too.'

And then he stiffened, as if that thought surprised him. He shifted on his chair. 'Are you close to *your* parents, Wynne?'

She had to answer—tit for tat. It was only fair. But it occurred to her that sharing such intimacies, while innocuous on the surface, might lead to deeper intimacies. She swallowed as temptation coiled about her in ever tighter circles. She sensed that she needed only to give Xavier the smallest of signs and he would kiss her.

One tiny sign…

Her mouth dried. What was she *thinking*? Xavier was nothing like any of the men she'd previously dated, and for that reason alone she needed to stay well and truly out of his way—she'd be out of her depth with him. Besides, what if she took the chance and things went badly? It would put everyone's jobs in jeopardy. She couldn't risk that.

Xavier leaned in and his sudden closeness chased a thrill across the surface of her skin even as fear tripped ice down her spine. Not fear of what he would do, but of what *she* wanted to do—she wanted to drag his head down to hers and lose herself in him completely.

There's too much at stake!

YOUR PARTICIPATION IS REQUESTED!

Dear Reader,

Since you are a lover of our books – we would like to get to know you!

Inside you will find a short Reader's Survey. Sharing your answers with us will help our editorial staff understand who you are and what activities you enjoy.

To thank you for your participation, we would like to send you 2 books and 2 gifts – **ABSOLUTELY FREE!**

Enjoy your gifts with our appreciation,

Pam Powers

SEE INSIDE FOR READER'S SURVEY

For Your Reading Pleasure...

We'll send you 2 books and 2 gifts
ABSOLUTELY FREE
just for completing our Reader's Survey!

YOURS FREE!

*We'll send you two fabulous surprise
gifts absolutely FREE, just for trying
our books!*

YOUR READER'S SURVEY
"THANK YOU" FREE GIFTS INCLUDE:
- ▶ 2 FREE books
- ▶ 2 lovely surprise gifts

PLEASE FILL IN THE CIRCLES COMPLETELY TO RESPOND

1) What type of fiction books do you enjoy reading? (Check all that apply)
- ○ Suspense/Thrillers   ○ Action/Adventure   ○ Modern-day Romances
- ○ Historical Romance   ○ Humor   ○ Paranormal Romance

2) What attracted you most to the last fiction book you purchased on impulse?
- ○ The Title   ○ The Cover   ○ The Author   ○ The Story

3) What is usually the greatest influencer when you <u>plan</u> to buy a book?
- ○ Advertising   ○ Referral   ○ Book Review

4) How often do you access the internet?
- ○ Daily   ○ Weekly   ○ Monthly   ○ Rarely or never

5) How many NEW paperback fiction novels have you purchased in the past 3 months?
- ○ 0 - 2   ○ 3 - 6   ○ 7 or more

YES! I have completed the Reader's Survey. Please send me the 2 FREE books and 2 FREE gifts (gifts are worth about $10 retail) for which I qualify. I understand that I am under no obligation to purchase any books, as explained on the back of this card.

119/319 HDL GLNV

FIRST NAME

LAST NAME

ADDRESS

APT.#

CITY

STATE/PROV.

ZIP/POSTAL CODE

READER SERVICE—Here's how it works:

Accepting your 2 free Harlequin® Romance Larger Print books and 2 free gifts (gifts valued at approximately $10.00) places you under no obligation to buy anything. You may keep the books and gifts and return the shipping statement marked "cancel." If you do not cancel, about a month later we'll send you 4 additional books and bill you just $5.34 each in the U.S. or $5.74 each in Canada. That is a savings of at least 15% off the cover price. It's quite a bargain! Shipping and handling is just 50¢ per book in the U.S. and 75¢ per book in Canada.* You may cancel at any time, but if you choose to continue, every month we'll send you 4 more books, which you may either purchase at the discount price plus shipping and handling or return to us and cancel your subscription. *Terms and prices subject to change without notice. Prices do not include applicable taxes. Sales tax applicable in N.Y. Canadian residents will be charged applicable taxes. Offer not valid in Quebec. Books received may not be as shown. All orders subject to approval. Credit or debit balances in a customer's account(s) may be offset by any other outstanding balance owed by or to the customer. Please allow 4 to 6 weeks for delivery. Offer available while quantities last.

◄ If offer card is missing write to: Reader Service, P.O. Box 1867, Buffalo, NY 14240-1867 or visit www.ReaderService.com ◄

BUSINESS REPLY MAIL

FIRST-CLASS MAIL   PERMIT NO. 717   BUFFALO, NY

POSTAGE WILL BE PAID BY ADDRESSEE

READER SERVICE
PO BOX 1867
BUFFALO NY 14240-9952

NO POSTAGE
NECESSARY
IF MAILED
IN THE
UNITED STATES

'Where on earth did you just go?' he demanded. 'So many emotions fired across your face I could barely catch a single one of them.'

'Good,' she croaked.

His eyebrows lifted.

'It never does for a woman to be an open book.' She made the riposte in an effort to lighten the mood, but it didn't help.

She grabbed the jug and refilled his glass, tried to gather her scattered wits. Easing back, she tucked a strand of hair back behind her ear. 'You asked about my parents…I have no idea who my father was. I'm not sure my mother ever knew either.'

We were ships in the night, darling—that was what she'd always been told.

'Does that not bother you?'

She could tell that it would bother *him*. 'Not any more. I went through a stage in my teens when I wanted to know, but…' She shrugged. 'I eventually came to the conclusion that if he'd cared so little about my mother then he probably wouldn't have cared too much about me either.'

He didn't say anything in answer to that, so she pushed on.

'I love my mother, but she doesn't have a maternal bone in her body.'

He frowned. 'I do not understand.'

'I mean she had me, and then discovered she much preferred being a free spirit. She found it limiting to have a baby tying her down.'

Wynne hadn't been enough for Coral. She'd tried hard not to take it personally.

'It was a relief all round when she finally left me with my grandmother and moved on to greener pastures. She's currently being a free spirit in France.'

'How old were you when she left you with Aggie?'

'Five.'

'And yet you still love her?'

That was the difference between them—he would resent something like that forever. 'My grandmother has been the real maternal figure in my life. I've not lacked for love, Xavier. My mother has been more like…an aunt.'

He nodded slowly. 'So you love her, but perhaps you do not respect her. At least not in the same way that I respect my parents.'

She braced her hands on the table. 'If I ever have a child and the best they can say about me is that they *respect* me, then I'll feel as if I've gone wrong somewhere.'

He blinked.

She folded her arms. 'Please tell me you mean to demand more of yourself in the parenting stakes.' Her heart started to thud and she didn't know why. 'Do you mean to send Luis away to boarding school?'

He stiffened. 'This conversation has become far too personal.'

He could say that again!

He swiped a hand through the air. 'This is not where I meant for our discussion to go.'

She folded her arms. She knew that revealed her defensiveness, but she couldn't help it. He *made* her defensive.

'You had an agenda for our conversation?' she asked.

She watched him war with himself, and eventually he drew away, slid back behind that impervious mask. She told herself she was glad of it.

If only her gladness didn't feel so much like disappointment.

'You accused me earlier of treating you like an enemy, and you were right. I'm sorry for that.'

Oka-a-a-y. In her mind Wynne drew that word out. It was an expression of regret rather than an apology, but she was happy to roll with it. For now.

'And yet I cannot help feeling that there is something you are worried that I will do…something in relation to the motel that you would fight tooth and nail against.'

Bingo.

'I would like to know what that is.'

If she told him would he use it against her?

She leaned towards him. 'Xavier?'

'*Si*?'

'Correct me if I'm wrong, but this is my afternoon off, is it not? I don't talk shop in my leisure time any more—boss's orders.'

She seized her glass and drained it. When she set it back down she found him glaring at her.

'Now you are…how do you put it…? Fudging… fencing with me?'

'Being obtuse,' she agreed. 'I would argue, however, that work wasn't the conversational agenda you originally had in mind.'

His glare deepened. 'You know not of what you talk.'

That was another thing. Whenever he grew uncomfortable his grammar suffered. Well, far be it from her to shy away from an awkward topic—she'd acknowledge it, get it out in the open, and move on.

She pulled in a breath. 'I think it had something to do with the fact that I kissed you. I think what you really want to tell me is that I overstepped the boundary and to not let it happen again.' She shot to her feet. 'Well, you don't have to worry. I…'

Her words petered out as he rose and leaned so far across the table her mouth went dry. Desire drew maddeningly lazy circles across her skin.

'Then you would be wrong.'

His eyes flashed, but the finger he trailed down her jaw to where the pulse pounded in her throat was gentle. He idly toyed with the sensitive flesh there, his finger moving back and forth until the breath jammed in her throat.

'Wrong?' she croaked.

'I wanted to determine if…'

A breath shuddered out of her. 'If…?'

'If you would be amenable to overstepping those boundaries further.'

He couldn't mean that!

'Oh, but I do,' he murmured, and she realised she'd said the words out loud.

He leaned in so close his breath fanned across her lips. She could feel herself sway towards him. She wanted him so badly exactly *because* he was so different from the men she usually dated. He wouldn't want anything from her. He wouldn't ask her to introduce him to someone who would further his career. He wouldn't want her to mollycoddle him.

She broke out in gooseflesh. He'd be an amazing lover.

'You are a beautiful, desirable and sometimes baffling woman, Wynne. I want to make love with you.'

She bit her lip to keep from saying, *Yes, please*!

'And I do not think you would take much persuading.'

She let his words sink in. He thought her so desperate and needy that she'd fall into his hands like a ripe plum? She opened her mouth, but his finger against her lips halted her words.

'I do not say that because I am arrogant. I say it because I recognise that there is a spark, a heat between us. You can refuse to acknowledge it if you wish, but ignoring it won't make it go away.'

They stared at each other. She was sure he must hear the thud of her heart.

'So I accepted your offer of a drink with the intention of…'

She held up a hand and nodded. 'But then you thought better of it?'

Before she could tell him she applauded his wisdom he drew himself up, his eyes flashing fire.

'You told me I was a bad father! I will *never* send my son away!'

She rocked back. 'I did no such thing.' She went over her earlier words. 'You've completely misinterpreted what I said. I meant that I believe you would prefer to have a relationship with Luis that is closer to the one you and Lorenzo shared rather than the one you have with your parents.'

They stared at one another in silence for a long moment, until Wynne nodded to break the spell that threatened to wrap around her.

'But you were right—our conversation did become far too personal. I shouldn't have said such a thing. Be assured that from now on I'll mind my Ps and Qs.'

His nostrils flared.

'And, while there might be heat between us, if I recall it correctly you don't *fraternise* with your staff.'

His chin lifted. 'For you I would make an exception.'

She couldn't afford to be his exception.

Why not?

Um...

This man addled her brain, but instinct told her to retreat. Becoming lovers didn't mean they'd become friends. She needed the security of friendship before she entered into anything deeper with this man. Never again would she set herself up to be told she wasn't *good enough*.

'As you say, there might be a spark—but it doesn't follow that every spark should be lit.'

He didn't answer.

'I don't think you like me very much,' she added.

He opened his mouth, but she pressed on.

'And, while I respect you, I'm not sure I like you very much either.'

His lips pressed together into a tight line that turned them white. 'I see.' His nostrils flared. 'You have made your position very clear. I'm sorry if I have made you feel uncomfortable. If you'll excuse me, I have phone calls I need to make.'

He strode across her yard and disappeared through the gate. She collapsed back down to her chair, but it took a very long time before her heart stopped pounding.

CHAPTER SEVEN

LUIS ARRIVED THE next day. Given what had passed between him and Wynne the previous afternoon, Xavier had been tempted to delay his son's arrival for another few days. But he ached to see him. And in his heart he knew Wynne would not treat Luis with anything but kindness.

And, as he'd known she would, she made sure she was in the foyer when Reyes returned from his trip to the nearby airport with Luis and Paula to welcome them personally to Aggie's Retreat. *Villa Lorenzo*, he silently amended.

Xavier's heart lifted at his first sight of his son. He had spoken to Luis every day on the phone, but it didn't make up for seeing him in the flesh. Especially when Luis had grown so uncommunicative of late.

A frown shuffled through him when Luis didn't come racing into the motel as fast as his legs would carry him and hurl himself at Xavier. So, instead, Xavier strode forward to seize Luis beneath the armpits and toss him above his head.

'I have missed you, Luis.' He kissed his cheek.

'I missed you too, Papà.'

He said it formally, and it stung. What had happened to make Luis so withdrawn and reserved? Did he blame Xavier for Camilla's absence from his life? He bit back a sigh. He'd hoped a few days of sightseeing—of enjoying the zoo, the amusement parks and ferry rides—would lift his son's spirits. It obviously hadn't worked. But then only a fool would think that fun and amusement could make up to a child for a mother who'd proved false—a mother who'd turned her back on him.

Luis was suffering and the knowledge broke Xavier's heart.

He turned to Wynne, letting Luis slide down to the ground. 'Wynne, this is my son. And this is his nanny, Paula.'

'I'm not sure I like you very much.'

All night her words had tormented him. He'd tried to tell himself that it didn't matter what she thought of him. Except...it seemed it did.

Wynne sent a smile to Paula, and then she actually knelt on the carpet in front of Luis, so as to be on the same level as the four-year-old.

She held out her hand. Luis stared at her with big eyes. In Spanish, Xavier told him to shake Wynne's hand. Instead of shaking his hand, though, Wynne seized it and pressed a kiss to the palm, which almost surprised a smile from Luis. *Almost.*

'Luis, I swear you're so cute I could just gobble you up. Speaking of gobbling... Have you had one of these yet?' She pulled something from her pocket. 'This is one of the best chocolates in the whole world.'

She handed a bright wrapped sweet emblazoned with a cartoon koala to Luis. He stared at the candy bar in awe, then at Wynne, and then, to Xavier's absolute amazement, he grinned.

'*Gracias,*' he murmured shyly, before holding the candy bar up so Xavier could see it.

Xavier tried to make the appropriate noises of wonder that were expected of him.

Laughing, Wynne rose to her feet. 'I'll let you into a little secret, Luis. I have a huge jar of those in the kitchen. So you let me know when you need another one, okay?'

Without warning, Luis grabbed Wynne's hand. 'Would you like to hear a song?'

Wonder briefly lit her eyes, and something in Xavier's chest jangled when her face softened.

'More than anything in the world.'

And Luis sang her a song! It wasn't a song Xavier had ever heard him sing before.

When he was finished, Wynne tucked his hand inside her own with a smile that could light a ballroom. 'Luis, I can tell that you and I are going to be the very best of friends.'

That wasn't part of the plan!

She led him towards the drawing room. 'Would you like to learn a *new* song?

Luis nodded eagerly, and Xavier was left staring in bemusement after them.

* * *

Over the course of the next few days Luis chatted to Wynne and Tina with a total lack of reserve. He played rowdy games of cricket with Blake and Heath, and the sound of their laughter and the healthy glow in Luis's cheeks lightened Xavier's heart. But Luis grew quiet and solemn whenever he was alone with his father. And when Xavier questioned him Luis swore that nothing was wrong.

Something *was* wrong, all right. It was just that Xavier didn't know how to get to the bottom of it.

Xavier strode down the stairs to check on Luis. Paula had a migraine and he'd ordered her to take the rest of the day off to rest. Wynne and Tina had set Luis up with some books and toys in the drawing room.

Tina glanced up, but her smile faltered when she saw him. It put him on his guard. 'What is wrong?'

'Nothing. Luis is in the drawing room.' She picked up the phone as if she needed to make an urgent call. 'He's been as good as gold.'

From the foyer windows he could see Wynne exchanging pleasantries outside with the florist's delivery driver. And then he watched her fish out her phone, glance at the number, and then glance back towards the motel.

Had Tina just rung her?

What on earth…?

Without waiting to hear any more half-truths or obfuscations, he strode into the drawing room. He came to an abrupt halt when he saw that Luis had a playmate. His heart started to thud as he watched Luis order the girl to do something or other with the blocks they were playing with. She said something back that he didn't catch, and their shared laughter made something in his chest twist.

Wynne almost barrelled into him when she came charging into the drawing room a moment later. She somehow managed to sidestep him with a funny little, *'Oomph.'* The scent of jasmine rose up all around him.

She righted herself and sent a cheery greeting to the pair on the floor. 'Hello, Luis. Hello, Libby.'

Both heads shot up from where the children played between the sofas and the television, the coffee table having been moved against the wall.

'Miss Wynne, come and see what we've built!'

She moved across to them, and it left Xavier feeling stranded.

'Wow! You've built a city? That is the best! You sure you guys did all that on your own?'

Luis grinned and nodded. *'Sí.'*

The girl opened her mouth, closed it, and then shrugged as her innate honesty came to the fore. 'Luis did most of it. But I helped—didn't I, Luis?'

'Sí, Libby helped a lot.'

Libby had Down Syndrome, and her...*difference* didn't seem to faze Luis in the slightest. The realisation had pride puffing through Xavier's chest.

He didn't want his son judging others because they were different. He didn't want him to be afraid of that difference. He wanted his son always to display kindness and acceptance.

Wynne glanced at Xavier, as if trying to judge his reaction at finding Luis playing with the girl. Did she think he'd be angry? *Dios!* What kind of man did she and Tina think him?

Wynne held up the flowers. 'Libby, look what's arrived.'

Libby scrambled to her feet and clapped her hands. 'Mrs Amini's flowers! I'll go put them in her room right now. Can I? I got the vase ready before…I'll be really, *really* careful.'

Libby was a *housemaid*? It took three beats before the deeper implications of that sank in. Before acid started to burn his stomach…the back of his throat. It was all he could do not to drop his head to his hands.

'Yes, you can. But first come and meet Mr Xavier—the new owner of Aggie's Retreat.' She turned to Xavier. Her eyes had turned murky… cloudy…but she tilted her chin at a defiant angle. 'Xavier, this is Libby—one of our housekeeping staff.'

'I'm very pleased to meet you, Mr Xavier.' Libby spoiled the effect of her polite formality when she grinned up at him. 'You have the best motel in the *whole* world and I *love* working here.'

Her smile was so wide and guileless it almost broke his heart.

'Thank you, Libby. It is a great pleasure to meet you.'

'Okay, here are the flowers.'

Wynne handed them to Libby, who took them reverently.

They watched her take the stairs slowly. Only when she'd disappeared from view did Xavier turn back to Wynne. In his chest, his heart pounded. *Damn it all to hell!*

'I expect you now have some point to make?' he said.

She knew that in the culture of luxury he wanted to create here there would be no place for the Libbys of the world. And that knowledge burned at him. He recalled Wynne's passionate, *'That's not a world I want to live in.'* Now he understood why.

He'd bet Libby was just the tip of the iceberg.

He dragged a hand down his face. Wynne had built something unique here. Something good. Did he really have it in him to destroy it?

Lorenzo deserves the best!

'A point to make?'

Wynne shrugged and, he suspected, chose deliberately to misunderstand him.

'You want to know about the flowers? One of our regular guests—Mrs Amini—once let slip how much she loved pink and yellow carnations. So whenever she stays we make sure to have a bunch in her room. Believe it or not, she now drives half an hour out of her way, since her sales route changed last year, to stay here. She's sent at least three of her fellow salespeople to us.' She shrugged. 'It's a nice way to do business.'

'That's not what I meant and you know it.'

But perhaps, in a roundabout way, it was. She was telling him that the people who stayed here—and the people who worked here—were just as important as the high-flying clients he had in mind for The Lorenzo. And he would agree with her. It was just…

Lorenzo deserves the best!

She swallowed, gripping her hands together. 'Would you like me to write you a report?'

Turmoil rocked through him. 'No.' Not that he expected her to heed him. He could practically see her mentally drafting the said report.

'Tía Wynne, can Libby play with me again tomorrow?'

Luis had taken to calling Wynne *tía*—aunt. For some reason that made Xavier's chest clench up even tighter. So did the brilliant smile that Wynne sent his son.

'I'll see what I can arrange, pumpkin.'

She made her smile wide enough to encompass him as well. 'Enjoy your afternoon, gentlemen. I'll see you both at dinnertime.'

And then she left, leaving questions he couldn't answer pounding through him.

He glanced at Luis. 'Can I play?'

Luis shook his head. 'It's finished now. And I know you are very busy and have a lot of work to do.'

Dios! Nobody wanted his company—not even his son.

For the next week and a half Wynne only saw Xavier at brief moments throughout the day and at dinnertime. He'd said he wanted time to go over all of the motel's records and account books. He'd said he was busy running the rest of the Ramos hotel empire, and that Aggie's Retreat was small fry as far as he was concerned.

She didn't believe that last bit—it had been said to put her in her place. She'd worked out that he called the motel Aggie's Retreat when he was being critical, and Villa Lorenzo when he was being complimentary.

He'd told her simply to get on with the job he paid her to do.

And she didn't blame him for that. Not in the slightest.

Way to go, Wynne. Tell your boss you don't like him. What a winning move!

She didn't know how to unsay it, though. Not without revealing that she'd said it deliberately to create distance between them because she found him far too tempting.

On Monday—eleven days after her ill-advised

'*While I respect you, I'm not sure I like you very much either*' comment—she was waltzing down the corridor with seventy-year-old Horace Golding when Xavier called her in to the conference room.

She forced herself to beam at him. 'Horace has been waltzing me down that corridor since I was fifteen years old.'

Xavier pressed the fingers and thumb of one hand to his eyes and she knew in that moment that today was D-Day—the day the motel's fate would be decided.

She collapsed into the chair opposite, and they faced each other across the table like opponents. With hands that shook, she opened her laptop. She opened a new document and then went to her recent browsing history and selected 'Hostage Negotiation Techniques'. It didn't seem too over the top. It *felt* as if Xavier were holding the motel to ransom.

The first instruction read: *Don't be direct*. Apparently that could come across as aggressive and rude.

Okay. Um…

She smiled at Xavier. 'Can I get you any refreshments? It'd only take a moment to put the coffee pot on.'

He shook his head. Then he frowned. 'Do *you* want coffee?'

'No, I'm fine.' She wasn't sure her stomach was stable enough even for water.

Don't be direct.

'I hope everything has been going well in the Ramos hotel world? You've been flat chat.'

'Flat chat?'

'Busy.'

Suspicion flitted across his face. 'Are you hoping to hear that my corporation is about to fall over?'

'No!' She stared at him, her heart dashing itself against her ribcage. How could he have so badly misinterpreted her? 'Dear Lord!' She pressed a hand to her chest. 'That'd be a disaster. Think of all of those jobs lost! It doesn't bear thinking about. That would be very unwelcome news for Ag—Villa Lorenzo.'

He glared. 'So why ask?'

'I…uh…' Her mouth went dry. 'I was just making small talk.'

She glanced at her screen. Tip number two: *Get them to say no, not yes*. Saying yes would apparently make him feel trapped. Phrasing a question that he could answer in the negative would apparently make him feel safe.

Oka-a-y.

She looked up at him. 'But of course you don't pay me to make polite small talk, do you?'

She tried to accompany her words with a smile, though she feared it was a weak effort.

He stared at her, and for the briefest moment she thought he might smile. 'That's not strictly speaking true.'

No! You're supposed to say no!

'Your ability to make small talk with the guests at the motel is a valuable skill.'

His words shocked her so much she said, 'You think I can be an *asset* here?' And then she realised what she'd done. 'No, no—don't answer that.'

The frown in his eyes deepened. 'Why not?'

'Because it sounded like I was fishing for a compliment, and I'm quite certain that's not the point of this meeting.'

Which begged the question—what *was* the point of this meeting? She couldn't ask outright because that would be *too direct*.

Tip three: *Let them feel in control*. He *was* in control! Ah… But did he feel he was the one setting the agenda? Or did he feel she was railroading him?

She opened her mouth—*Don't ask a direct question*. She closed it again. *Argh!*

'Wynne, do you feel all right?'

No! Her head was spinning so fast her temples had started to throb. 'I'm fine. Truly,' she added at the look he sent her—a Look with a capital L.

She glanced at her computer screen for help. *Defuse the negative*. Which she was supposed to do by acknowledging what she thought he'd perceive as all the negatives in relation to his dealings with her. *Uh-huh*. She swallowed. Did he have all day?

'Look, Xavier, I know I must seem difficult to work with. And maybe you think I haven't been listening to you closely enough on how you want this motel to be a fitting tribute to Lorenzo. But I truly only want to help you make that dream a reality.'

As long as I get to keep my staff.

He sat back. 'I appreciate that.'

She glanced back at her computer. There were two tips left. Somehow she had to get him to say the words *That's right*. Once he said those words it would indicate that he felt she understood him.

She panicked for a moment, then suddenly stilled. 'You loved your grandfather. You want to create a place that he'd be proud of.'

'Yes.'

Could that be interpreted as *That's right*?

The final tip advised her to *Play dumb*. The article gave her examples.

She swallowed and nodded. 'How can I help you do that?'

She couldn't read the expression in his eyes and it took all her strength not to fidget under his gaze.

'That is what this meeting is about,' he said finally.

'Okay.' She nodded, and hoped her expression looked winningly open.

'Wynne, are you sure you feel okay? You look… odd.'

'Just nervous,' she confessed, her shoulders slumping. She tried to stiffen them again.

'Why?'

'Because I suspect you must think me cold and

rude, not to mention unfriendly. And…' She grimaced. 'It makes me feel…'

'Nervous?'

Was he laughing at her?

'This is because of what happened in your back yard eleven days ago, yes?'

'Um…yes.'

'I do not think you are cold or rude or unfriendly.'

Why didn't she feel reassured? 'Okay, then. That's a relief.'

'Anything else?' he enquired.

She couldn't help feeling his felicity was faked. 'Did you know that Aggie would've loved to turn this place into a luxury hotel?'

He didn't so much as blink. 'Then she won the wrong venue.'

His words didn't make sense.

'I have considered what you said to me after we visited the Golden Palace. I have considered many options.'

Her heart thundered up into her throat.

'For the moment I do not mean to pursue the option of turning this place into a luxury hotel.'

Her mouth opened and closed. 'So…no demolition?'

He shook his head.

Direct or not, she had to ask the question. 'Do you mean to close us down?'

His head rocked back. 'Absolutely not.'

She sagged.

'So that is why you've been acting so odd?'

She sent him a weak smile. 'It was one of the options that had been passing through my mind.'

'Lorenzo wanted to buy this place back. He didn't want me to destroy it.'

That was something, at least. As long as the motel was a going concern, then she could continue to advocate for her staff. 'That's good news.'

He shook his head again, as if the conclusion she'd jumped to completely baffled him. 'I want to make changes, yes. Significant changes. I want the entire motel refurbished—I want a complete revamp of the decor—I want to expand into budget romantic getaways. But you have created a consistent and loyal clientele. I do not want to lose their business.'

She sat up straighter. He was giving them a chance to prove themselves! 'Would now be a bad time for me to tell you what I see as the motel's strengths?'

Finally he smiled. It wasn't a big smile, but at the moment she would take whatever she could get.

'No.'

He'd said no! She was getting better at these negotiation techniques.

'Now would be a very *good* time to tell me what you see as the motel's strengths. We can compare notes and see if we're on the same page.'

It suddenly occurred to her that Xavier's negotiating techniques were far, *far* stronger than her own.

* * *

An hour later, Xavier sat back and studied Wynne. He had a razor-sharp mind and comprehensive business acumen, and he hadn't slowed down to let her catch up. But, while she might lack a university business degree, he hadn't needed to. She'd kept up with him effortlessly. She was wasted here.

In the interests of both cost and efficiency, Xavier had been all set to standardise the décor, basically making all the rooms carbon copies of each other. She'd argued—gently—against that. Apart from its laudable hospitality, Aggie's Retreat's biggest draw-card was its eccentricity. The personalisation that was evident in the hospitality extended to each guest was also reflected in the individuality of the rooms.

According to Wynne, her regular guests had favourite rooms that were given to them whenever possible. She'd argued that it created a sense of ownership, of investment…a sense of truly feeling that this was a home away from home. She'd illustrated her argument with guest testimonials and reviews.

It might not be the way a Ramos luxury hotel was run, but the demographic at Aggie's Retreat was very different from what he was used to—and he was starting to see that Wynne's guests truly wanted different things from what his signature hotels offered.

He found that difference invigorating.

'So let me see if I have this right.' Wynne punched

keys on her laptop. 'You don't have any…appreciation for this twee Victorian manor house décor, do you?'

'I do not.'

Her lips twitched and, as ever, her mirth proved contagious—though he tried to keep his answering amusement under wraps. She'd told him in no uncertain terms that she wasn't interested in pursuing anything romantic with him. He *would* keep his distance.

'But you don't dislike the idea of making over the motel in a Spanish theme?'

'I do like that idea.' It seemed somehow symmetrical.

'Then let me wow you with this splendidness.'

She turned her computer towards him—and she *did* wow him.

He pulled the laptop closer to flick through the files she'd created. 'How did you pull all of this together in so short a time?'

Colour bloomed high on her cheeks. 'Oh, I…' Her gaze slid away. 'I thought I'd work on it a little in the evenings and I…'

She trailed off with a shrug. Was she sleeping as badly as he was?

'I guess I got carried away.'

He glanced from the files back to her. 'This has to have taken longer than the odd hour here and there.'

She'd created exact replicas of the motel rooms using a computer-assisted drawing program, but rather than copying their current English Victorian incarnations she'd decorated them in a Spanish-Moorish style.

There were rounded arches in place of squared fretwork. Arabic calligraphy and decorative tiles abounded. The themes and colours changed from room to room. In one room there was a decorative sofa with ornate carvings and inlays, in another a Persian rug in hues of blue and cream. Cedar chests, high-backed chairs with ebony-coloured inlays, beds hung with rich brocade, tapestries on the walls, tooled leather, silver braziers—the rooms had been created in such fine detail he could almost smell them!

'Wynne, this is extraordinary. You have a remarkable eye.'

She rubbed a hand across the back of her neck, still not looking at him. 'You have to understand that for many years now I've played with different ideas for redecorating the motel. It's been a bit of a…hobby.'

Suddenly he understood. 'But this, perhaps, has made you feel you are not being quite true to your grandmother?'

Her head shot back. 'Absolutely not! You don't know how wrong you are.'

He didn't think he *was* wrong. There was something about her manner that didn't ring true…something altogether out of character with her usual openness. He didn't pursue it. She was entitled to her secrets.

'So, given this hobby of yours, when you found out the prospective new owner was Spanish…?'

She stared doggedly at the computer screen. 'There didn't seem to be any harm in playing with some ideas.'

'No harm whatsoever. I like these ideas a great deal. Can we get costings for the work as soon as possible?'

'Absolutely!' She started to push her chair back. 'Would you like me to get on to it now?'

'No.' He might have given up on the idea of creating something splendidly luxurious, and transforming the motel in homage to Lorenzo *was* long overdue, but there was one more matter they needed to discuss. 'I want to talk to you about your staffing arrangements here. I've read over all the files.'

The colour drained from her face. Her stricken expression knifed through him. She obviously thought him completely without a heart.

He watched her master her dread…or at least the appearance of it. In its place she donned an expression of careful interest and an attitude of deference that set his teeth on edge. He steepled his fingers and counselled himself not to snap at her.

'You currently employ Libby, along with two other part-time housemaids and two part-time gardeners from a local shelter.'

'That's right.'

'You feel that their slower efficiency rates are worth the public service you are providing to the wider community?'

'We receive government subsidies for hiring from the shelter, so there are sound business reasons underpinning that decision. I mean, we can't afford to carry staff who don't pull their weight—this is a business, after all.'

Behind the clear green of her eyes he sensed her mind racing.

'It's true,' she added, 'that Libby and her cohorts might be a little slower than other workers, but it's equally true that they get through the work. They're not shirkers.' Her face softened. 'They're also inspiringly cheerful—not to mention grateful for the opportunity to work. It makes for a very happy working environment.'

Wynne had created a family here. Her mother might have abandoned her, but she'd created a home for more than just herself. His stomach churned. She must have been in dire straits to jeopardise all that and sell to *him*. No wonder she lived in fear of him destroying it.

'It's also true that Libby and her fellow workers need to be supervised very carefully. But April—who you might recall is—'

'Your head of housekeeping, yes.'

Did she think he paid no attention whatsoever? Did she think he held himself so far above his staff that he didn't even know their names?

The fact of the matter was the moment he'd met Libby he'd known that he'd have to abandon his dream of creating a luxury hotel. Villa Lorenzo would have to become something else—and it had taken him several long, dark, sleepless nights to find any peace in that conclusion.

It had helped him to know, instinctively, that Lorenzo wouldn't want him to create a hotel where workers like Libby weren't welcome. But what *would* Lorenzo have wanted? How could Xavier pay a fitting tribute to Lorenzo…commemorate his grandfather's memory in a lasting and worthwhile way?

What would Lorenzo have wanted?

He'd have wanted Xavier to accept that afternoon tea that Wynne had organised as a welcome for him.

The shock of that realisation had made Xavier's stomach pitch. *'Don't make the same mistakes I made.'* Lorenzo would want a place where he could be himself—a place of fun and whimsy. Most of all he'd want any sign of coldness, superiority and disapproval banished.

Wynne cleared her throat, and Xavier pulled his thoughts back to the here and now.

'Well, April is very experienced, and she's excellent with all the housemaids.'

'You do not hire your breakfast girl, Meg, from the shelter?'

The pulse in her throat pounded, betraying her agitation. 'You've noticed Meg's scars?'

He had. 'How did she come by them?'

'Her ex-boyfriend threw battery acid at her.'

He dragged a hand down his face.

'I hired Meg from an agency that places women who are victims of domestic abuse into the work-force.'

He glanced up to see her rubbing a hand across her chest.

'I hired Tina from the same agency.'

His hand clenched. Men had hurt these women...?

Wynne glanced at his fist and swallowed hard. He forced himself to relax it.

'I am very sorry that Meg and Tina have had such bad experiences.'

She tossed her hair, her eyes growing dark and defiant. 'And I suppose you also ought to know that I hired both April and Justin, our maintenance man, from prison release programmes.'

He straightened. 'They are...*criminals*?'

She pointed a finger at him. '*Ex*-criminals, who have paid their debt to society.'

Her finger shook. He wanted to reach across and kiss it.

'Xavier, you can turn away from people like this all you want. It doesn't change the fact that they exist. When you turn your back on the chance to help—on the chance to make a good difference in the world—then you become part of the problem.'

He hadn't turned his back on anyone, and her as-sumption stung. 'It's is not my responsibility to—'

'Of *course* it is! How much money do you make? What opportunities in life have you been granted that other people can only dream about? Of course you have a responsibility! You and everyone else like you who enjoys a privileged position.'

'Did I say that I would not work with the staff you have employed here?'

Her throat bobbed. 'You mean…?'

'So this is what has had you so worried all this time? You have been afraid that I will not work with such people as Libby, Meg or April?'

She stared at him with throbbing eyes. 'It would be easy for someone like me to start over, Xavier, but *far* harder for them.'

She *did* think he had no heart!

'So feel free to fire me, if you must, but—'

'I have no intention of dismissing you!' The words left him on a roar. He had no intention of dismissing *anyone*!

She leaned across the table towards him, suddenly earnest. 'If it makes any difference whatsoever, this programme is totally my own idea. I'm the one who implemented it—not Aggie.'

She thought *that* would have an effect on his decision? She thought he would punish innocent parties because of *Aggie*?

His stomach churned. But wasn't that exactly what he'd been intending to do? However unknowingly?

He shoved his chair back. 'The staff can stay.'

She stared at him as if a giant weight had been lifted off her. 'Oh, Xavier! I—'

'I believe you have enough work to be getting on with for the rest of the day, yes?'

The brilliance of her smile faltered. 'Yes, of course.'

'Then I'll leave you to it.'

He stalked from the room, trying to out-stride the darkness threatening to settle over him.

CHAPTER EIGHT

XAVIER STOOD OUTSIDE of the doors of the Clover Fields Care Home on the outskirts of town the following Wednesday afternoon and eased a breath from his lungs.

If Wynne knew he was here… Well, she'd be far from pleased. But, regardless of what she thought, he had no intention of yelling at Aggie. He had a message to deliver. And then he would leave.

Once he'd done this, and the refurbishment on the motel was complete, he could return to Spain. The sooner that happened the better. He dug his fingers into the tight muscles of his nape, trying to shift the tension that had him wound up tight. Wynne and her treating everyone like members of a happy family was starting to get to him. It was all very pleasant, but it was still a fantasy. He had to leave before he started to believe in it.

Because, regardless of what Wynne said, she didn't like him. She didn't think he had a heart. She thought he represented everything that was the antithesis of the culture she'd created for the motel. Despite her smiles and her dinners and all her good humour and hospitality, her 'happy family' ethos didn't include *him*. And *that* stung more than it had a right to. The problem was that she was so adept at creating that impression there were times when he was in danger of forgetting it was just a fantasy.

At least with Camilla he hadn't been in danger of falling for a fantasy so far out of his reach.

And meeting Aggie today would help break that spell too.

Without giving himself any further time to think, he pushed through heavy double doors. Discreet enquiries had informed him not only of the name of Aggie's nursing home, but her room number as well. He stood outside her door for a couple of moments before forcing his legs through the doorway.

An elderly woman glanced up from the bed, her eyes bright. 'Do I know you, dear?'

She was *tiny*! He came to a dead halt and his heart started to pound. Bile churned in his stomach. He'd built Aggie up in his mind as some kind of Amazonian temptress without a heart. But the woman in the bed was so frail and…human. And old!

'Are you my father?'

He stilled and a fist tightened about his chest. 'No.' He swallowed and cleared his throat. 'I'm a…a friend of Wynne's.'

'Wynne?' Her eyes clouded. 'I don't know anybody by that name.'

'Your granddaughter?'

'I have a granddaughter?'

He closed his eyes. *Oh, Wynne.* His heart went out to the younger woman for all she'd been silently suffering.

* * *

A familiar voice floated from Aggie's room into the corridor and Wynne stopped dead a few steps short of the door.

Xavier!

She went to leap forward, but at the last moment forced herself back. She couldn't go racing into Aggie's room, grab Xavier by the throat and shake the living daylights out of him—no matter how much she might want to. It would upset Aggie—frighten her—and Wynne had made a promise to herself to make these final years of Aggie's as happy and comfortable as possible.

She'd kick Xavier *and* his butt to kingdom come once they were away from here. Except…

She edged forward to listen more closely.

'I'm going to have to draw again.' That was her grandmother's voice, thick with petulance.

'You just want all the tiles to yourself. I'm on to your tricks.'

Aggie wheezed out a laugh.

Wynne blinked. Xavier was playing *dominoes* with Aggie?

'I used to be good at this game. I used to be very beautiful too.'

'You're still very beautiful. And, while you might be good, I might be even better.'

Aggie chortled. 'Listen to him! Typical man.'

Wynne's eyes filled. She recognised that voice—

and that spirit. She saw so few flashes of it these days…and every single one of them was precious.

Blinking hard, she pulled in a breath and made herself enter the room. Aggie sat up in bed, dwarfed by all her pillows, while Xavier sat at the foot of the bed. The meal table on its castor wheels stood between them, spread with dominoes. Xavier glanced around and—*the devil*—didn't even have the grace to look uncomfortable. The compassion in his eyes made her want to sob.

'Your grandmother has been wiping the floor with me at dominoes.'

'Glad to see you haven't lost it, Nanna.'

She kissed Aggie's cheek and settled on the other side of the bed from Xavier, their shoulders momentarily brushing. It sent a jolt of heat through her that had her sucking in a breath and wishing she'd chosen the chair instead. Except the chair was on Xavier's side of the bed, his knee almost touching it, and it seemed too close, too familiar—too dangerous—to seat herself there. Besides, she had no intention of giving him such a height advantage over her.

She pulled a cellophane bag tied with red ribbon from her purse. 'Carmen sent you a packet of those fancy-schmancy marshmallows you love so much from that little place up the coast.'

Aggie cradled the packet reverently before loosening the ribbon and sticking her hand in. She pulled forth a sticky concoction and popped it straight in her mouth.

Her grandmother might occasionally be unsteady on her feet, but she could still open a bag of sweets quicker than anyone Wynne knew.

Xavier's lips twitched as he watched Aggie. 'Good?'

Aggie crushed the bag to her chest. 'Get your own!'

Her smile had turned to a glare of suspicion.

Wynne glanced at her watch. It was nearly six in the evening. 'Sundowning' was what the staff called it. She didn't want Xavier to witness this. So far he'd obviously been polite, even kind to Aggie. The older woman didn't deserve his scorn and condemnation. She didn't deserve him to see her at her worst.

Wynne turned to him, doing her best to control the pounding of her heart. 'I know you're a busy man, Xavier. Please don't let us hold you up any longer.'

He pursed his lips and she held her breath. She was almost certain that he was about to nod and make his goodbyes when a marshmallow hit Wynne in the ear.

Xavier's head rocked back.

Perfect.

'Don't you try and chase my suitors away, you hussy!'

She couldn't look at him then, her stomach curdling at the picture that she and Aggie must make. She plucked the marshmallow from her hair and dropped it to the table before sliding the table out of her grandmother's reach. She didn't want to give the older woman the chance to send it hurtling on its castors at her or Xavier.

'You're right, Nanna. That was a little clumsy of me.'

She prayed her soothing tone would appease Aggie.

'When is Carmen coming to visit? When is she going to take me home?'

Carmen? Wynne knew that Aggie had simply plucked the first name she could recall from the air, without rhyme or reason, but it still jolted her. And she still couldn't look at Xavier. She couldn't bear to see what his face would reveal—his pity… and perhaps his triumph.

'Carmen is in Sydney at the moment, with her little grandson.'

'You tell her to return right now!'

'I'll pass on the message.'

'Get me my phone. I'll call her. She'll listen to me. You're—'

'Lorenzo sends his love,' Xavier suddenly broke in.

Aggie stopped her tirade in mid-sentence, her mouthing hanging slightly open. 'Lorenzo?'

Xavier nodded.

'What did he say?'

'He asked me to give you these.' He pulled out a playing card—the Queen of Hearts—from his pocket, and a shiny penny piece. 'He wants to buy the motel back.'

Aggie took the card and pressed it to her chest. 'Really?'

Xavier crossed his heart.

'Can I see him?'

Xavier hesitated. 'He's a little poorly at the moment, which is why he couldn't come himself.'

She stared at the playing card, at the shiny penny, and then she kissed them, tears running down her cheeks. 'He was so angry with me...but this means he's forgiven me.'

'Forgiven you?'

It was Wynne who asked the question. Her heart pounded as she waited for her grandmother to answer.

'I wanted him to stand up to his family and stay here with me. I tried to force his hand. So I won the motel...' She tossed her head. 'He accused me of stealing from him when I never did! But...I let him think it.'

Wynne's eyes filled. 'Oh, Nanna.'

'I told him when he came to his senses he could buy the motel back with a penny...and an apology.'

Her gaze, sharp and momentarily lucid, fixed on Xavier. 'You look like him.'

Xavier swallowed and nodded. 'He told me how beautiful you were. I had to come and see for myself.' He lifted her grandmother's hand to his lips. 'And now I know he wasn't exaggerating.'

Her grandmother chuckled. 'You, sir, are an outrageous flirt.'

'So are you,' Xavier shot back, making the older woman cackle with laughter.

CHAPTER NINE

A NURSE TRIPPED into the room with a cheery, 'It's time to take your medication now, Ms Stephens.' And the Aggie Wynne knew and loved disappeared again.

Aggie grabbed Xavier's hand. 'They're trying to kill me. So's she.' She pointed a finger at Wynne.

'Now, now...' The nurse tut-tutted. 'We'll have none of that.'

Aggie's distress tore at Wynne. She leapt forward and took the older woman's hand. 'Oh, Nanna. I'll stay until—'

Aggie reefed her hand away. 'You're a wicked, bad girl. You call me Nanna, but you've left me in this place to rot!'

A torrent of invective followed.

A second nurse came into the room and ushered Wynne and Xavier out. 'Leave her to us now. We'll make her comfortable.'

Wynne couldn't speak for the lump in her throat. She just nodded and set off down the corridor. Xavier kept pace beside her. She wished him a million miles away. And yet at the same time she had to fight the temptation to press her face into his shoulder and draw comfort from his solid strength.

Once outside, he reached for her hand, but she twisted away. 'Don't even think about it!'

'Wynne, I—'

'You should be ashamed of yourself!'

And yet he had made Aggie laugh. For a short time he'd cajoled the old Aggie out from beneath the confusion that bedevilled her.

'I am.'

His sober admission annihilated her outrage. She stumbled across to a bench and collapsed onto it. From here there was a view of the Gold Coast hinterland, but darkness had started to fall and all she could see were house lights as they came on.

He took the seat beside her. 'Go away, Xavier.'

'I do not wish to leave you when you are so upset.'

'*I* don't want you thinking dreadful things about Aggie, but we don't always get what we want.'

He reached out again and this time took her hand. She should shake it off. Instead she found her fingers curling around his.

She turned to him. 'I know you've been outraged on Lorenzo's behalf, but to hunt down an eighty-eight-year-old woman to taunt her with something that happened fifty-five years ago—it's wrong.'

He glanced down at their linked hands. 'I didn't go to taunt her, Wynne. I promised Lorenzo I would deliver his message. I promised to put that card and the penny into her hands.' He shook his head. 'I got everything wrong. She loved him.'

Silently she acknowledged that Xavier wasn't

guilty of the cruelty she'd accused him of. She'd misjudged him. His grief and his anger had made her suspicious—and she refused to feel guilty about that—but Xavier hid a kind heart behind that steely façade.

She sagged back against the bench. She'd misjudged him about the staff. And now it appeared she'd misjudged his motives towards Aggie.

'But, even though my motives were not unkind, I realised the mistake of turning up to see Aggie unannounced the moment I walked into her room. What right did I think I had to rake up a fifty-five-year-old chapter in her life?'

Even in the dim light she could see the self-reproach that raked him.

'I knew that before she spoke—before I realised that she had…'

'Alzheimer's Disease,' she confirmed for him.

'I am sorry, Wynne. I would apologise to Aggie too, if I thought it would do any good. But I fear it would only confuse and agitate her.'

Wynne swallowed the lump in her throat and ignored the burning at the backs of her eyes. 'You were very kind to her. You took the time to entertain her. I'm not happy that you came here today, and I won't pretend otherwise, but I can't accuse you of cruelty. It seems I've misjudged you…again.'

'Again?'

He watched her so closely it made her pulse jump. 'I thought you would take against my staff, but you didn't. I should've given you the benefit of the doubt.' She swallowed. 'I'm sorry.'

'You do not need to apologise to me.'

She tried to smile, only her lips refused to co-operate. 'It's very difficult, this situation with Aggie, but that doesn't absolve me of admitting when I'm wrong and apologising for it.'

He stared at her with dark throbbing eyes, but didn't say anything.

This time when she tried to smile, her lips co-operated. 'You're now supposed to accept my apology.'

'Of *course* I accept your apology!'

'And I want to thank you for making Aggie laugh. For a little while she sounded like her old self…and that's a gift.'

'And yet you still wish I hadn't visited her?'

His perception took her off-guard and she suddenly realised she held his hand so tightly her nails dug into his skin. She let go and tried to pull her hand away, but he refused to relinquish it.

'You absolve me of cruelty towards your grandmother, but you still wish I hadn't come. Why?'

She couldn't contain her agitation. 'Because now all you're going to see whenever you think of Aggie is that petulant, angry, venomous woman, who hurls abuse at her granddaughter and is paranoid about the nurses. You're never going to know the woman she was—the real woman who was my grandmother. The woman who apparently loved your grandfather.'

'Then tell me about her.'

His hand was warm and encouraging, and he bumped shoulders with her gently in a gesture of comradeship...friendship.

And so she did.

She told him how loved and secure Aggie had always made her feel, and of the fun they'd used to have together. She told him that Aggie had treated Wynne as a gift, and never a nuisance—as if being given the chance to raise her had been an honour rather than an imposition. She told him of Aggie's kindness and how she'd helped people—*really* helped them.

She told him of the spectacular and sometimes outrageous parties Aggie had thrown, her equally outrageous flirtatiousness and the cocktails she'd adored—which had usually featured *crème de menthe*.

'She always had time for a chat. Not just with me, but with everybody. Her attitude to life was so... *positive*. It's why the guests loved her, and why so many of them remember her fondly still.'

'And that's the reason you decided to follow in her footsteps?'

Xavier's hand anchored her. It felt right—which was crazy—but she left her hand there all the same, loath to spoil the moment.

'She was over the moon when I told her I wanted to run Aggie's Retreat. I mean, she'd saved up enough money to send me to design school because she thought that was what I wanted, but running Aggie's Retreat was my dream—there's nothing else I've ever wanted to do.' She glanced up at him. 'Likewise, Lorenzo must've been delighted when you said you wanted to run the Ramos Corporation with him.'

'It is hard to say. Everyone just took it for granted that was what I would do.'

Did duty always come first for Xavier? 'Was there anything else you ever dreamed of doing?'

His lips lifted. 'When I was Luis's age I wanted to be a fireman. And a little later I wanted to be a professional footballer. But as I grew older I simply...' He shrugged. 'I simply wanted to work with Lorenzo.'

She nodded. 'I wanted to be just like my grandmother. I'm not. I don't have her flamboyance. But I love Aggie's Retreat every bit as much as she did.'

He let out a long breath, his nostrils flaring. 'Then why did you sell it?'

The lump she'd almost conquered lodged back in her throat, making it ache with a fierceness that had her eyes filling.

'Oh, Wynne...'

The soft whisper of her name sent a shiver across her skin. She wanted to ask him to keep talking in that same low tone and never to stop.

His fingers tightened about hers. 'You sold the motel to cover her medical bills?'

His words were heavy, and an answering heaviness descended over her. She leant against him and he brushed a kiss to her hair. A pulse started up inside her. She should move back, but she doggedly pushed away the voice of caution sounding through her.

'The truth is once my grandmother is gone I'm not sure I'll have the heart to remain at Aggie's Retreat—or Villa Lorenzo—or whatever other name it might go by.'

'But what will you do?'

She had no idea. 'Start afresh, maybe, somewhere new.'

'But your family is here—at the motel. Wynne, you are just as loved there as Aggie ever was. You *belong* there.'

Did she? She wasn't sure any more.

'I feel as if I betrayed them.' Her eyes burned and she stared at their linked hands as if they could somehow save her. 'Tina, April, Libby and the others. I put Aggie's welfare above theirs. I can't help but think they must secretly resent me.'

'They love and admire you.' He cupped her face, turning it until she met his gaze. 'They know the struggles you have had. You are tired…and depressed. It is understandable. But never doubt your own worth or the value of what you do. I, for one, think you are an amazing woman. And I am not alone in that evaluation.'

Funnily enough, it wasn't anybody else's evaluation she was interested in at the moment—only his. It shouldn't matter so much—what he thought of her. She shouldn't *let* it matter so much.

She gave a shaky laugh. 'My grandmother was right—you're a dreadful flirt.'

He stared down at her with such intensity—as if to force her to see the sincerity of his words—that her breath stuttered in her chest.

'I am not flirting, Wynne. This is not an attempt to flatter you. I mean what I say.'

His perfect lips uttered the words perfectly, and need rose up through her with a speed that made her gulp. His eyes settled on her lips and darkened before once more shifting to meet her gaze. His thumb brushed across the pulse-point of her throat as if he couldn't help it, making her blood leap beneath his touch.

She swallowed, her mouth drying in a combination of heat and desire.

'I think you are the most amazing woman I have ever met and I do not know what to make of it.'

Her heart hammered and her eyes filled. 'Xavier, please don't toy with me. Here—at this place—' Her limbs had grown too heavy to gesture at the long, low building behind them, but she knew he understood what she meant. 'I have no defences here. It…this place…it makes me too vulnerable and—'

His finger touched her lips and her words trembled to a halt.

'I do not toy with you. For my own peace of mind I wish I could say that I were.'

The words rasped out of him and she realised he felt as vulnerable and at sea as she did. She didn't have the power to put him away from her. She had no desire to do anything of the kind. And she knew the same fever gripped him.

His eyes flashed—not with anger, but with passion. 'Tell me to let you go and I will.'

She reached up to cup his face then. 'You create such a fire in me I fear I'm burning up.'

His head swooped down and his hands tilted her head until his lips captured her in a kiss that burned itself onto her very soul.

Wynne clung to him to keep her balance, to keep herself together, as everything within her soared free. The insistent warmth of his lips sent heat swooping and dancing through her. She tried to kiss him back with the same slow, terrifying intensity, but his kisses made her too hungry, too greedy for patience and restraint.

Thrusting her fingers in his hair, she pulled him closer and closer, opening herself up to him until she felt the last of his resistance shatter and he swept her onto his lap, his mouth moving over hers with a fervour that left no room for thought…only feeling and relishing and wondering…

'Dios!' He wrenched his mouth from hers, breathing heavily. 'I wanted to know if you would taste like lemons or caramel.'

She blinked, his words barely making any sense. 'Your voice…the things you say…can be both tart and sweet. But you do not taste of anything so commonplace. You taste like spring sunshine in an orange grove, and the wind that flies before a summer storm, and the deep stillness of a winter's night when the stars are at their most brilliant.'

Nobody had ever spoken to her in such a way before. Nobody had ever kissed her in such a way.

He swallowed. 'If I do not stop this madness soon I will be in danger of forgetting that I am a gentleman.'

She didn't want him to stop. She sucked her bottom lip into her mouth. He watched, his arms tightening about her, his gaze ravenous. She could still taste him there—a thrilling, illicit flavour that couldn't be good for her.

'Nobody has ever kissed me like that before,' she whispered.

His eyes glittered in the darkness. 'Then they have been fools.'

She lifted her chin. 'Kiss me again.'

It wasn't a request, but a demand, and with a low chuckle he did.

He pressed kisses to the corners of her mouth, nipping and teasing until she writhed with a need that bordered on madness. Finally she captured his face in her hands and held him still while she explored every inch of his mouth. When she traced the inside seam of his lips with her tongue the restraint in him snapped and he tugged her close, kissing her so deeply she never wanted to surface.

Hands on her shoulders eventually pushed her back, and she found herself lifted bodily out of his lap and planted none too gently back on the bench.

'Do you want me to lose all sense of myself and our surroundings?' he growled at her, leaping up to pace a short distance away before coming back.

His eyes glittered and she could practically sense the leap of his blood beneath his skin. She'd done *that* to him?

He flung an arm out. 'Do you want me to tumble you to the ground in a public place and have my way with you? Is *that* what you want?' He glared at her.

She lifted her chin, but didn't stand. She wasn't sure her legs were steady enough to support her. 'I take exception to your phrasing, Xavier. It could just as well be *me* tumbling *you* to the ground to have *my* wicked way with *you*.'

He didn't smile. 'A gentleman always takes care of his lover.' He fell back to the bench beside her. 'Would you dare kiss me like that—with so much abandon—if we were alone at your cottage?'

In a heartbeat!

Though she didn't say that out loud.

His words did give her pause, though. Xavier was unlike any man she'd ever met. If she pushed him beyond his limits there would be consequences.

The thought made her break out in goosebumps.

'You made me feel wild, free, reckless.' He made her feel she could be anything she wanted.

A low laugh rumbled out of him. '*Mi tesoro*, your

kisses were wild and reckless. You could make a man forget himself.'

They stared at each other.

'Let me take you out tonight—for dinner and dancing.'

It was the last thing she'd expected him to say.

'No expectations,' he added carefully. 'It does not mean that I expect to end up in your bed at the end of the night.'

It might just be that was exactly where she wanted him, though. Her pulse went mad.

What if he tells you you're not good enough?

But what if he doesn't?

'I would just like to take you out.'

'Why?' she managed over the pounding of her heart.

'Because I think now that I like you.'

Warmth flooded her.

'And I think, perhaps, you know now that you like me too.'

She nodded.

'We have cut through the worries and resentments that have constrained us. That makes me happy.'

'So you would like to celebrate our…better understanding?'

His lips tightened. 'I have been difficult to work with. And you…you have had a lot to put up with on top of dealing with me. I would like to make amends.'

He felt *sorry* for her?

'Also, I would like the chance to kiss you again.'

'Sold!' She grinned as excitement shuffled through her.

He frowned. 'Does that mean yes?'

'It's a resounding yes.'

He hesitated. 'Wynne, I do not wish to give you a false impression.'

She stilled. 'Meaning…?'

He took her hand and pressed a kiss to her wrist. 'My marriage cured me of any desire to make a lasting commitment to any woman.'

Her wrist throbbed and tingled. 'And you think that's what I want?'

'I do not know…and I wouldn't dare make any such presumption.'

His qualification made her smile. He'd obviously been paying attention when she'd told him that he might want to rethink the way he phrased his words.

'But you tell me you're a good girl. So…'

'It's true. I am. That doesn't mean I'm ready to settle for slippers and a hot water bottle just yet.'

A fling with Xavier might be foolish, but it had been so long since she'd had anything but work and worry in her life. She craved the excitement, the temporary rush, the sheer headiness that being with him gave her.

'I'll make a deal with you. I promise not to be cruel as long as you promise not to be a no-hope loser.'

His smile made her soul sing. 'You have my word.'

She moistened her lips. 'There's something else we need to settle. You're the boss and I'm...not.'

His nostrils flared. 'I would never use my position to coerce you into—' He halted at her raised hand.

'I know that. But can you promise me that regardless of what happens this evening—or doesn't happen—it will have no impact on the staff at the motel?'

'You have my word of honour.' His chin lifted. 'I have already made the decision to keep your staff, Wynne. I have no intention of changing my mind.'

She believed him. Honour meant something to this man.

She pulled in a breath. She'd secured the safety of her staff's jobs; her grandmother was safe. Surely that left her free to follow the reckless impulses of her heart.

'Wynne?'

Excitement and resolution balled in her chest. 'You're not looking for commitment, but that doesn't mean you don't enjoy the company of women, right? I would *love* to go out with you tonight.'

He smiled and it stole her breath.

'Woman,' he corrected. 'Tonight I'm only thinking of a single woman, Wynne, and that's you.'

The promise in his words made her toes curl.

'I will meet you in the motel's foyer at eight, yes?'

She glanced at her watch. It would give her just enough time to shower and dress. 'Yes.'

He seized her hand before she could scurry off to her car. 'Tonight, Wynne, is all about what *you* want. I promise.'

She didn't do anything as prosaic as walk to her car. She floated.

He took her to a fancy beachfront tapas bar where they ate finger food and sipped cold beer from bottles. He looked dark and dangerous in black dress trousers and a navy shirt. The flash of his smile and his deep laugh turned him into a seductive pirate. All he was lacking was a gold earring.

The appreciation that gleamed in his eyes when they rested on her made her glad she'd gone to the effort of donning her gladdest glad rags—a silk sheath dress in a riot of colour that slid across her skin in feather-light caresses whenever she moved.

When their plates were cleared away, she said, 'Tell me about your ex-wife.'

'Why?'

'Curiosity,' she said, praying her shrug was a study in carelessness. 'And you did say tonight was all about what *I* wanted, so I thought you might allay my curiosity. I take it she was one of these cruel women you find yourself drawn to?'

The lines at the corners of his eyes crinkled upwards. '*You* are not a cruel woman. Maybe my taste is improving.'

She stared down at the twinkling tea light enclosed in a mosaic glass holder. It sent flickers of red and blue dancing across the table. If he didn't want to talk about Camilla, she wouldn't force the matter.

'How old are you, Xavier?'

'Thirty-six.'

'I'm thirty-three. And look—' she opened her arms wide '—not a no-hope loser in sight. Maybe we've both reached a crucial stage in our personal development.'

He reached out to trace a finger down her cheek. 'You are worth far more than you give yourself credit for. Promise me that you will not waste yourself and your time on these men who are not worthy of you.'

His eyes impelled her to say yes. She swallowed. 'I'll do my best.'

'Promise me. You are a woman who does not give her promises away lightly. Give me your word.'

She hesitated, and then nodded. 'I promise.'

Her reward was a brief kiss pressed to her stunned lips. Despite its brevity, it left her tingling all over.

Xavier's gaze lowered, and then his eyes gleamed and colour rose high on his cheekbones. Wynne glanced down to see her nipples peaking through the thin silk of her dress. Heat flushed up her neck and into her face, and she had to fight the urge to fold her arms to cover her chest.

He reached out and took her hand, as if sensing her embarrassment. His smile was so slow and so full of sin her heart started to hammer.

'Would it be of any comfort if I told you that you have the same effect on me?'

She stared at him, and then she smiled. 'That's a very great comfort.'

He stared at her mouth as if mesmerised, before shaking himself and shifting on his chair. 'I was going to take you to the casino once we were done here. I thought it would be amusing to give you a handful of chips to fritter away at roulette.'

'Casinos are fun.' It was hard to form words when everything inside her had grown so tight with need. 'But I don't hold with gambling.'

'There is no problem as long as one does not gamble away more than one can afford to lose.'

It suddenly seemed as if there were a subtext to this conversation, but she couldn't quite grasp it. Talk of gambling, though, had her mind turning to Aggie and Lorenzo.

'Camilla and I had been dating for eight months when she became pregnant with Luis.'

The fact that he'd decided to answer her previous question momentarily threw her. 'Were you in love with her?'

'I was very taken with her, but I do not believe I was ever in love with her. Still, I was fully prepared to commit myself to her for life.' He traced his finger around the candleholder. 'And you do not have to be in love with someone for them to have the power to hurt you.'

That was true enough. 'What happened?'

'I was very pleased that we were expecting a child.' He went silent, his lips briefly turning white. 'She told me that if I didn't marry her she would abort our baby.'

That was emotional blackmail! It took a moment before she trusted her voice enough to speak. 'So you married her.'

'It did not seem like such a bad idea. She always made me laugh, and would very often do things with the object of pleasing me. I lavished her with attention and gifts, and escorted her to the society events that she so loved. I have known marriages based on less compatibility.'

Compatibility? Where was the passion and excitement, the romance?

'What happened?'

'Once we were married, and Luis was born, she gave up all pretence of liking me.'

She rocked back, shocked. 'If she didn't like you, why did she marry you?'

He shrugged, but she sensed the pain behind it.

'I expect she wanted the position in society that being my wife would give her. I believe she deliberately became pregnant to make that happen.'

'That's appalling!'

Not to mention foolish. To have Xavier and then throw him away—the woman must have rocks in her head!

'I completely misjudged her. And when I finally

saw her for what she was I realised I'd married a woman like my grandmother.'

She leaned towards him. 'Lorenzo's wife?'

'Yes.' His nostrils flared. 'My grandmother was seemingly proper and respectable, but she had a cold heart and a sense of superiority that could make one feel humiliated and insignificant. She made Lorenzo's life hell.'

Her heart burned. Poor Lorenzo. And poor Xavier, witnessing his grandfather's heartbreak at such a young age.

'When I realised the resemblance between Camilla and my grandmother I could not stand to remain married to her another second. And, as she never showed the slightest interest in Luis, I felt no compunction in offering her a financial incentive to sign custody of Luis over to me.'

'You've never prevented her from seeing Luis, though?'

'No.' His lips thinned. 'But she does not take the trouble to see him often. She makes dates with him and then cancels at the last moment. *Dios*, I sometimes think she is worse than no mother at all!'

Her heart hurt. 'You took a gamble that things would work out between you and Camilla, but your gamble didn't pay off.'

In the flickering candlelight shadows danced in his eyes. 'Luis's happiness was the stake—and those stakes were too high.'

'You are not to blame.'

'But nor am I blameless.'

Her heart started to thud. 'There's something I have to tell you.'

He frowned. 'This is something I will not like?'

'I hope you won't take it too much to heart. It was sort of in fun…' She winced. 'But it was a little mean.'

He raised an eyebrow. 'Cruel?'

She drew herself up. 'Absolutely not! We couldn't have that or you might fall for me!'

He laughed, as she'd meant him to, but she found her own laughter becoming strained. That joke had started to wear thin.

'It must also be pointed out that I was provoked.' She swallowed. 'The thing is, Xavier, I have to confess that the theme for the motel—the Spanish theme that I wowed you with—that was Aggie's dream. That's why my drawings are so detailed and…and gorgeous. The two of us have been plotting to turn Aggie's Retreat into a Spanish oasis since I was a little girl. If she'd had the money, Aggie would've renovated the place in a heartbeat.'

He sat back—away from her.

Her heart thudded and her stomach churned. 'Are you awfully angry with me?'

Slowly, he shook his head. 'No, but…'

'You're shocked at how well I can lie, aren't you? I'm an excellent liar. I've always been able to keep a straight face.'

He reached out to curl a finger around a lock of her hair. Inside her a pulse started to pound.

'It is not that. As you pointed out—you were provoked. The opportunity to put me in my place would, I suspect, have been irresistible to your sense of...*fun*.'

She grimaced.

'Your grandmother and my grandfather—they loved each other.'

'Yes.'

'It is sad that their falling out prevented them from being together.'

'And yet if they had married we wouldn't be here.' She glanced down at the candle. 'It seems Lorenzo's family didn't approved of Aggie. Family pressure—family duty—can be hard to resist.'

'True, but it can be resisted.'

'But if Lorenzo was so angry with Aggie... thought she didn't love him...' She bit back a sigh. 'I *so* wish she'd gone after him.'

'And yet, as you say, if she had we would not be here now.' He tugged gently on her hair. 'And I am *very* glad I am here with you now.'

CHAPTER TEN

TOUCHING HER HAIR was not enough. He wanted to touch all of her. He forced his hands back to the table, away from temptation.

She sent him a smile. 'It does no good to dwell on a past we can't change.'

As she spoke a tightness in his chest loosened, and then it slipped away. He should say something, but he found it hard to concentrate on words. His attention kept snagging on the frosted shine of her lips and the way the material of her dress moved across her body whenever she shifted on her seat. Lust and need coursed through him, leaving him ragged…and oddly energised.

The high colour on her cheekbones told him he'd been staring.

'Stop looking at me like that, Xavier.'

His fingers ached with the need to touch her. 'Like what?'

She slanted him a smile that had his blood smouldering.

'Don't be coy. You know exactly what I mean. The way you've been looking at me should come with an R-rated warning.'

Even through the haze of desire she could make him laugh. Her own glances had been shyer than his, and more circumspect, but the attraction she felt for him was unmistakable. Her every stolen glance felt like a caress against his skin.

He leaned in closer and dragged a breath of jasmine-scented woman into his lungs. 'Would you dance with me?' His skin ached with the need to hold her close.

'Yes…'

Her breathlessness speared straight to his groin. He started to rise.

'But not in public.'

He fell back into his seat, his heart hammering.

'I have a smooth jazz album at home, and an equally smooth Scotch.' Her eyes held a challenge. 'Would you care for a nightcap?'

His pulse thundered in his ears. 'Are you *sure* about this?'

'Oh, I'm *very* sure, Xavier.'

He didn't say anything—just called for the bill.

Dawn had only just started to break—nothing more than a faint glow through the window—when Wynne's alarm dragged Xavier from sleep. She clicked it off, turned back to press a soft kiss to his shoulder—an action that flooded him with warmth—then attempted to slide out of bed.

He reached out and seized her about the waist, and pulled her naked body back flush against his. The hitch in her laugh and the shiver that rocked through her pushed the last remnants of sleep from his mind. He scraped his teeth gently across her throat and she arched into the touch. He sensed her melting beneath him.

'Xavier...'

She turned in his arms, planting a hand to his chest, but rather than pushing him away her fingers explored, caressed...relished. Her palm grazed back and forth across one of his nipples.

'I...I have breakfasts to make.'

'Mmm...?' He nibbled her ear.

Her breathing grew satisfyingly ragged.

'And in about an hour you're going to have a little boy bursting into your room, looking for you.'

He grinned down at her. 'Then there's no time to waste.'

He couldn't get enough of this woman. He set his fingers, his mouth and lips, his hands, to exploring her every curve, until she arched up to him incoherent with need.

A short while later they lay side by side, breathing heavily.

'Good morning, Wynne.'

Her gurgle of laughter made him feel free. He turned his head on the pillow to find her smiling at him.

'That was incredible,' she said.

'*You* are incredible,' he told her. And he meant it. He'd never had such a lover. Wynne was so full of life and exuberance—and something else he couldn't define but that now he'd sampled it he craved it over and over.

It was why they'd made love three times last night.

And again just now.

A shadow passed across her face. 'I best grab a quick shower.'

She was gone before he could grab her wrist and ask if anything was wrong.

He sat up, the pillows piled behind him, ready for her when she returned—sadly wearing underwear beneath her robe. She dressed with no-nonsense efficiency. His gut clenched. Although she smiled in his general direction, her gaze didn't meet his.

He sat up straighter. 'Do you regret last night?'

She spun to stare at him. 'No!' She hesitated before coming to sit on the bed, just out of his reach. 'I had an incredible time with you last night, Xavier... and this morning. It's been amazing, but...'

Her frown made his chest burn. 'But...?'

She moistened her lips. 'It...our lovemaking...it was more intense than I expected.'

He froze. *Por Dios!* She hadn't gone and fallen for him, had she? He'd warned her—

'I think...I think it's best if we give each other a bit of space for a few hours...give the world a chance to return to normal for a bit.'

He wasn't sure he understood her.

'I'm just feeling a little overwhelmed.'

That he understood.

She smiled, as if to reassure him, but a horrible suspicion had started to form in his mind. Last night *had* been intense. *Very* intense. *Too* intense?

'Xavier, it's not stopping me from hoping that you're planning to stay in Australia for a good few weeks yet. So we can repeat last night's adventures over and over…and over.'

She leaned forward to give him a quick kiss and then she was gone. Her mischievous grin did nothing to ease the suspicion growing in his mind.

Was Wynne in danger of taking their affair too seriously?

With a curse, he flung off the bedclothes, dressed, and made his way back to his own room. Standing under the stinging spray of the shower a short while later, he told himself that he needed to call a halt to things between them. He could not toy with her affections.

He recalled the slide of her hands against his naked flesh…her eager kisses. They had inflamed him with a passion he'd never experienced before. The slide of her body against his…her softness contrasting with his hardness… He grew hard and hot, as if he'd been months without a woman.

Growling, he turned off the hot water and stood beneath the cold spray, willing it to chasten his flesh, willing his body back under control.

It took far longer than it should have.

Towelling himself off, he gave a hard nod. 'It has to end.'

Stalking into his room, he found that while he'd showered his breakfast had been delivered.

Wynne had given him an extra egg and an extra rasher of bacon. There was a note in a sealed envelope. He tore it open and read it.

Something to help keep up your strength. You're going to need it.

She hadn't signed it, but she'd drawn a smiley face. A very satisfied smiley face. He started to laugh. Perhaps they *could* risk another night. Or maybe a week. What harm could happen in a week?

He spent the next five nights in Wynne's bed.

He ordered her to organise additional staff so he could take her out in the evenings. He took her to the casino, and he'd been right—watching her lose at roulette and win at Black Jack was incredibly entertaining, not to mention incredibly sexy. In turn she took him and Luis to play mini-golf, and then for fish and chips on the beach.

Her laughter became as familiar to him as his own face.

That was when he realised he needed to start worrying. Not on Wynne's account, but on his own. He'd made it a rule not to become too comfortable, too familiar, with *any* woman. He had no intention of changing that rule now. Not for anyone. And Wynne understood that.

So on the sixth afternoon he tracked her down to where she was tidying in the drawing room, and made his excuses for that evening. He told her he had business in Spain he needed to attend to—phone calls he needed to make….time differences to take into account.

She simply smiled and nodded, his announcement barely rippling the surface of her customary cheerfulness. He'd readied himself for cajoling and pouting, perhaps even tears. Instead *she agreed with him*!

'We've been neglecting our duties shamefully. It's beyond time that I spent an evening with Aggie.'

Outrage he had no right to feel made him stiffen. 'You need not worry about preparing a meal for Luis and me tonight. I will make other arrangements.'

She leant back against the counter, folded her arms. 'Have I done something to upset you?'

The need to kiss her was so great it reinforced the wisdom of his decision to cool things down. 'Of course not.'

'Then why all this thunderous frowning?'

'Just…business worries. Nothing you need concern yourself with.'

She stared at him for a moment and then nodded. 'It must be hard running a business empire from a motel room. I suppose you'll be thinking of returning to Spain before too much longer.'

Dios! Did she want him gone?

'But I'm happy to cook dinner for you and Luis tonight. Especially if you don't mind eating a little earlier.'

'No, thank you.' He refused to force his company on her. 'We've imposed on you enough this week.'

Her lips twitched, that irrepressible twinkle making her eyes bolder and brighter. 'Is that what you call it?' she teased.

He couldn't answer. Something inside him had closed over.

She tilted her head, a frown in her eyes. 'Well... suit yourself.'

That was exactly what he meant to do.

The story broke in the tabloids the next day. The headline read: *The Billionaire and the Bleeding Heart!* and was accompanied with a huge picture of him and Wynne leaving an upmarket restaurant the previous Saturday night.

Xavier abandoned his breakfast to spread out the double-page news story on the desk. A hard fist knotted in his chest—a combination of anger at himself and anger at the parasitic journalists who sold other people's private lives for the world's entertainment. *El diabolo!* He should have taken more care. Why had he allowed himself to be lulled into a false sense of security?

The article linked him and Wynne romantically. It made it known that the two of them had been spotted at several trendy nightspots recently. It made much of Xavier's wealth and success and Wynne's social conscience. He hadn't known she campaigned for so many causes.

He studied the rest of the photographs, dragging a hand back through his hair. The desire and the heat that he and Wynne generated could not be denied. In one photograph Xavier was staring at her with such naked longing...and tenderness...he had to wheel away and pace the length of the room. How could he have let himself become so unguarded?

What on earth would Wynne make of this? What would she think? *He* was used to this kind of media scrutiny, but she was not. Would she read too much into it? His hands clenched. Would she take one look at that photograph and declare them officially an item now? A couple?

Bile burned the back of his throat. Obviously he would have to disabuse her of such a notion—if she held it—at the earliest possible opportunity.

He spun back to the desk and forced himself to read through the rest of the article. And as he did so the coldness inside him grew.

It appears that Ms Stephens has a weakness for playboys. Formerly linked with renowned artist and party-boy Duncan Payne, who rocketed to overnight fame and fortune when he won Australia's premier visual arts award, she has now set her sights on a bigger prize.

A small photograph revealed Wynne on a red carpet, smiling up into the face of a tall blond man. Xavier gripped the pages of the paper so tightly they tore.

She'd lied. She'd told him she was attracted to no-hope losers, but...

He stared at the photograph and swore savagely. She'd been stringing him along. All this time she'd been pretending to be honest and straightforward and caring and kind, but it was all a lie.

He recalled her lack of concern yesterday, when he'd said he couldn't spend the night with her.

Darkness threatened the edges of his vision. The whole time she'd been playing him. Just like Camilla had. And, just like Camilla, she probably didn't even *like* him! He'd thought she was different. He'd thought...

He frowned. No, it didn't make sense. If she didn't like him, what on earth would she get from a brief fling with him? Camilla had taken him for millions, but Wynne...

He stilled.

She'd not only got to remain working at the motel she loved, but was about to have it refurbished and modernised.

She'd safeguarded the jobs of the staff she felt responsible for.

She'd got to protect her grandmother.

His stomach twisted. He couldn't accuse Wynne of the same calculated cruelty as Camilla, but she'd had an agenda all the same. And she'd played him to achieve each and every one of her goals.

And he was a fool. *Again.*

His hands clenched. Well, no more. He could at least preserve a measure of dignity. Wynne could keep her position here, her staff could keep their jobs, and Aggie certainly need have no fear of him... But the one thing it was in his power to do was to call things off between them.

And the sooner he did that the better.

Wynne stared at the two-page spread Tina had all but dragged her to the front desk to see.

'Oh, for heaven's sake!' she muttered under her breath. 'Don't these people have better things to do than take pictures of Xavier and partner him up with every girl he has a meal with?'

'You're not dining out in this one.'

Tina pointed to a photograph of Wynne and Xavier walking on a moonlit beach...hand in hand.

Tina tapped the page. 'And look at how he's looking at you in this picture.'

'Don't go getting all starry-eyed on me.'

She made her voice tart, to counter the ache in her throat. This stupid newspaper article would give Xavier the excuse he needed to call off their brief... *relationship*—not that it deserved the word.

It had taken all her strength to feign nonchalance at Xavier's slowing of their affair yesterday. Everything inside her had rebelled at the idea. But she had her pride, and she *had* managed it.

She *still* had her pride.

She tossed her head. 'What's between me and Xavier is—'

'Yes?'

The deep, masculine voice with its stern, grim tone made both her and Tina start.

She'd been about to say *temporary*, but when she glanced up into Xavier's unsmiling face she silently amended it to *over*. She didn't need to be a rocket scientist to see 'end of the affair' written all over his face.

She forced herself to smile. 'Personal,' she said, very gently.

There was an unleashed violence in the set of his shoulders that she didn't want to let loose.

'Have you seen this?' She held up the paper.

His lip curled. 'Yes.'

Perfect.

She bit back a sigh. Turning briefly to Tina, she said, 'Can you chase up Bradford and Sons? If they won't give me a quote and a start date by close of business today, then tell them we'll be hiring someone else.'

Tina nodded. 'Roger.'

Wynne ushered Xavier towards the mercifully empty drawing room. 'I'm sorry, but Tina only just alerted me to the article so I haven't read it all the way through yet. Do you mind…?'

'Be my guest.'

But his every word came out clipped, and it was all she could do not to wince.

Or cry.

He was going to call it off. He was going to walk out of her life just when she was the happiest she'd ever been, and she didn't know how she would bear it.

You knew this would happen.

It was just… His lovemaking had been so tender and intense, and she'd started to think…

More fool you.

She pressed a hand to her forehead. An ending had always been inevitable, no matter how much she might wish otherwise. She'd been playing with fire and hoping she wouldn't get burned, but who had she been kidding? Her temples throbbed. It was never going to be possible for her to take a lover with casual unconcern and then simply move on untouched when the affair came to an end. She just wasn't built that way. And wishing otherwise had simply been a shield to hide behind, to hide from the truth—that she'd fallen in love with Xavier.

But she'd rather die than reveal that to him. He'd told her he didn't do long-term. He'd told her he didn't do love.

He'd told her!

The fact that she'd thought he'd been starting to care—

She shook her head.

Read the article.

She spread the newspaper out on the dining table, but she didn't sit because Xavier didn't sit. And she read. She huffed out a silent and somewhat bitter laugh. Trust them to mention Duncan. *Typical.*

'Okay.' She straightened when she reached the end. 'It's not too bad. It's all superficial nonsense, of course, but no outrageous claims have been made.'

His eyes flashed. 'No outrageous claims?'

She gestured to the paper. 'It's all speculation on the journalist's part—along with an attempt at…at titillation. There's nothing here, at least not that I can see, that will be harmful to either one of us or harmful to business.'

The cynicism that stretched across his face had her chafing her arms in an attempt to rub the sudden chill away.

'I expect you'll view such publicity as beneficial to business?'

She stared at him. 'You can't think I had anything to do with this?'

He shrugged, and the utter indifference of the gesture was like a knife to the heart. It was all she could do to stay upright.

'Who knows what goes on in the heart and mind of a woman?'

She fell back a step. 'I have no idea what you're blathering on about, but—'

'Blathering!' His brows snapped together and his hands clenched.

She recalled those hands moving over her body, sparking sensation and generating a passion she hadn't known existed, and had to swallow. 'I can assure you—' she kept her head high '—that I had nothing to do with that newspaper article.'

'Why should I believe you?'

The deceptively soft question punched the breath from her body. It took several deep gulps of air before she was able to answer. 'After everything we've shared you're going to question my honesty *now*?' A vice-like pain gripped her temples. 'You won't simply take my word for it?'

She'd thought him walking out of her life and never seeing him again would be the hardest thing she would have to bear. She'd been wrong.

'You warned me you were a good liar.' He raised one of those fatally sceptical eyebrows as his finger came down on the photograph of her and Duncan. 'It seems you twist the truth to suit your own purposes. This Duncan does not seem to be one of those…what did you call them? No-hope losers?'

He had to be joking!

'Duncan was the biggest no-hope loser of them all.' Her laugh held an edge she couldn't contain. 'He had nothing when I met him. *Nothing*. The agent who picked him up and launched his career used to be a regular here at Aggie's Retreat. I *introduced* them. Duncan dated me with the sole view of meeting that agent.'

Xavier's head rocked back, but his shock gave her no satisfaction. *This* was what he thought of her?

'When Duncan shot to fame and fortune he took his agent with him—but not me. His agent, I might add, wouldn't be seen dead staying anywhere as downmarket as Aggie's Retreat these days.'

'Why did he not take you with him?'

'Because I wasn't sophisticated enough, polished enough, or glamorous enough for his new world.' She folded her arms, acid burning a reckless path through her veins. 'You and Duncan have a lot in common, Xavier.'

She whirled away and made for the door, but then changed her mind and spun back. 'I knew yesterday that you were looking for a way to end things between us, but is this how you choose to do it—like this? By grabbing on to some stupid newspaper story and giving credence to its lies?'

She halted in front of him and slammed her hands to her hips. 'I knew things between us were only temporary, but I thought we could at least part as friends. I deserve more respect from you than that!'

She had to halt to pull a breath into her lungs. He opened his mouth, but she shook her head.

'I don't want to hear another word you have to say. I *liked* you, Xavier. I really liked you.' Beneath his tan, he paled. 'But you're barely human.' She tossed her head. 'I won't say any more now, for fear of being fired.'

This time when she made for the door she had no intention of stopping.

'I told you I would *not* dismiss you!'

The words were roared after her, but she didn't break stride.

Wynne sought the refuge of her cottage. She couldn't hide herself there all day, but she could nurse her anger and her hurt over a cup of tea before donning her armour and getting on with things.

But when she entered her yard she found Luis playing a disconsolate and solitary game of tether tennis.

She glanced at her watch—nine-thirty a.m. Why wasn't he with his nanny?

'Hello, Luis.'

When he spun round she saw he'd been crying. She held out her arms and he ran into them. She carried him over to the garden bench and let him cry.

She dried his face and cuddled him close. 'Do you want to tell me what's wrong?'

He snuggled into her. 'No.'

His voice was small and dispirited, and it caught at her heart. 'Would you like me to fetch Paula?'

'No!'

The tension that radiated through his small body made her frown, though she told herself to smile down at him. 'I'm your friend, Luis. I would never do anything to hurt you—you know that, don't you?'

He nodded.

'And because I'm your friend that means you can tell me anything. So can you tell me why you're sad?'

He glanced up at her and bit his lip. 'Paula tells me that I'm not to ask Papà to play with me—that he's very busy.'

She pulled in a breath. 'It's true that he's often busy, but your *papà* will never be too busy for *you*. He loves you. He loves you best of all in the world.'

Her young charge straightened. 'Really?'

She crossed her heart.

'Paula makes me promise not to tell Papà things.'

A chill chased itself up her spine. 'She shouldn't ask you to do that. You can tell your papà anything.'

'She tells me I'm not tell him that Mamà calls. She and Mamà say that if he knew he would put me in a home for bad boys.'

What? Wynne tried to swallow the anger that fired into her every cell. 'They're mistaken, Luis. Very, *very* mistaken. And do you know what? I can fix this.'

His face lit up.

'How do you feel about colouring in with Tía Tina for a little while?'

Wynne knocked on the conference room door. It was rarely closed, which probably meant Xavier wanted privacy.

Bad luck!

'Enter!'

The word was bellowed, and it was all she could do not to roll her eyes. She pushed into the room to find Xavier ensconced there with an agitated Paula.

'Luis has slipped away,' the nanny explained to Wynne.

'He's downstairs with Tina.'

'Oh!' She leapt up and started for the door. 'I will go to him at once.'

Wynne shut the door before the other woman could reach it. 'Take a seat, Paula.'

She glanced across at Xavier and ignored the burning in her chest. She told him all that Luis had just told her. When she'd finished she simply turned and left, closing the door behind her.

CHAPTER ELEVEN

PAULA'S SILENCE AFTER Wynne had left spoke volumes—ugly volumes.

Surely there were extenuating circumstances she could offer up? An explanation that a little boy wouldn't understand, but that an adult might?

None were forthcoming.

He paced the length of the room, his limbs cramping with the effort it took not to reach across and shake the woman. 'You have nothing to say?'

She glared at him. 'Camilla and I became friends. We bonded when Luis was just a baby…when you made her feel like a failure as a parent.'

He rocked back on his heels.

'So my loyalties lie with *her*, not with you.

A fist tightened about his chest. 'Shouldn't your loyalties be with Luis?'

'Camilla thought if Luis was afraid of you sending him away he would want to live with her.'

The back of his throat burned. 'You pair of—' He broke off, his hands clenching to fists.

She swallowed, and he realised she was afraid of him. It didn't displease him, but it gave him no satisfaction either. It was as if he could feel Wynne's voice inside his head, urging him to calmness—to focus on what was important rather than focussing on his anger and sense of betrayal.

He pulled in a breath. What was important at the moment was making Luis feel safe and secure again.

'You will pack your things and be ready to return to Spain immediately. I no longer require your services. I will have a driver here in fifteen minutes, and your tickets will be waiting for you at the airport. You will not go anywhere near Luis prior to leaving.'

She stared at him as if she couldn't believe that was all he meant to say to her.

'Go!' he barked, before he changed his mind.

She'd frightened his child, and a dark, primal part of him wanted to tear her limb from limb.

She leapt to her feet and fled.

Xavier organised the flight, and a driver, and then went in search of Luis.

He took him to the beach, and over the building of a sandcastle he told his son how much he loved him. He told him he would never put him in a home—that he wanted Luis to live with him always. He promised that solemnly.

He was careful not to say anything against Camilla.

At the back of his mind a question pounded—had he unknowingly made Camilla feel like a failure as a mother? He'd been so determined that Luis should not be reared with the same cold distance that he had that… Had he placed too much pressure on her? Had she withdrawn behind that icy hauteur as a form of defence? If so, why hadn't she said anything? Was he really such an ogre?

He dragged a hand down his face. Why had he not noticed? Why had he not questioned her more, rather than assume that she was as cold and uninterested in her child—and in him—as his mother and grandmother had been?

How much had his assumptions and his retreat behind a forbidding shield been responsible for today's revelation?

'Are you sad, Papà?'

He made himself smile for his son. 'I'm sad at the thought of you not living with me. I don't want that to ever happen.'

Luis flung his arms around Xavier's neck. 'I love you, Papà!'

'I love *you*, Luis.'

As his arms closed around the little body he swore that he would become the best person he could for his son.

Which meant at some point trying to make things right with Camilla too…

Xavier found Wynne checking the housekeeping stock with April a good two hours later. He asked her to step into the conference room for a moment.

Her lips curved upwards pleasantly enough, but her eyes told him to go to blazes.

Acid burned his stomach. She thought him an insensitive jerk.

He did his best not to notice her pallor, or the exhaustion that lined the fine skin about her eyes. 'I want to thank you for bringing Paula's duplicity to my attention.'

She picked imaginary lint from her skirt. 'You're welcome.'

'I had no idea that Camilla had recruited Paula in her plan to take revenge against me.'

She didn't glance up from her skirt. 'Revenge seems to figure large in your life.'

While her tone was pleasant, the words themselves were an accusation and they cut him to the quick.

He pulled himself up to his full height. He owed this woman. 'I can see you want to say something.'

'No, no...' she assured him.

'I'd rather you just...' He searched the air with his fingers. 'Spat it out.'

'Actually, I don't think you would.'

He thrust out his jaw. 'I insist.'

'Fine!' She tossed her glorious head of hair back behind her shoulders. 'Given what you accused me of earlier, I realise you must find it *astounding* that I should show so much moral fibre as to step in to help a little boy... Oh, to display such a lack of self-interest! But to tell you the truth, Xavier, I find that insulting.'

His every muscle stiffened in protest. 'That is not

so!' He wanted to *thank* her, not insult her. 'You have my gratitude. If it wasn't for you I would never—'

'Must I listen to this?'

The coldness in her eyes made him shrivel inside, but *he* was the person who had put it there. He found himself aching to bridge that distance.

'You were right. I latched on to Duncan and that stupid newspaper article as an excuse to call things off between us.'

That wasn't wholly true. He'd read about Duncan and he'd felt betrayed. He had no *right* to feel betrayed.

She folded her arms. 'Are you now going to try to resume our affair because I've helped you with your son?'

He attempted to quell the desire that gripped him, the hope that quickened his veins. He was in danger of becoming too attached. It wouldn't do. He couldn't allow it.

'No. It is best that we are no longer lovers.'

'I couldn't agree more.'

A fist lodged in his chest. He wanted to yell and tear things apart with his bare hands. Instead he forced himself to breathe deeply.

'But you were right. I should've treated you with more respect. I should've been honest with you.'

Some of the stiffness left her body. 'Honest?'

'The truth is I was worried you were becoming too emotionally involved. I have no desire to toy with your affections.'

Her mouth dropped open. His attention snagged on those lovely lips and hunger roared through him. It was all he could do not to stride around the table, pull her into his arms and kiss her.

Instead…

Instead she strode around the table towards him! *Por Dios!* If she kissed him…

Then he saw the fire—the anger—in her eyes, and he had to swallow.

'You want to know what I think?'

'Absolutely.' He nodded, though what he really wanted to do was flee from this room and not look back.

'What *I* think, Xavier, is that you're a coward! I think what you're really worried about is that *you've* become too emotionally involved.'

She was wrong!

'So, rather than call things off, like a normal person, you looked for reasons why I wasn't worthy of you.'

Not worthy of him? He simply hadn't wanted to hurt her. 'It was just supposed to be a fling!' he found himself yelling at her. 'No one was supposed to get hurt!'

Stop yelling at her! It's not her fault. She warned you. She told you she was a good girl through and through.

With Wynne he'd found himself out of his depth when he'd least expected it. As a lover, she'd been addictive—he hadn't been able to get enough of her. But he didn't *do* addiction.

She folded her arms and eased back. 'Are you saying I hurt you?'

His mouth went dry. 'Of course not.' Yet the thought of never having her in his arms again was pure torture. 'But it doesn't change the fact that I thought our affair was starting to mean too much to you—that *you* were in danger of being hurt.'

Her chin shot up. 'Even if that were the case, I made no demands on you.'

Maybe not, but he'd been afraid those demands would come.

She laughed, as if she'd read that thought in his face, and he winced at its bitterness.

'You think you're so sophisticated and urbane, so smooth and cultured, but you're not. You can no more do footloose and fancy-free than I can. You're too repressed to be a Jack-the-lad! You walk around as if you have a pole stuck up—'

'Enough!' She had no idea what she was talking about! And he would *not* descend to trading insults with her.

Her mouth snapped shut, but only for a moment. 'You act as if you're a class above everyone else.'

He did no such thing!

'With all your reserve and don't-touch-me detachment. But what makes you think that you're such a great catch anyway? Your wealth?' She wheeled away with a loud, *'Ha!'*

She made him sound like his grandmother!

She spun back. 'I guess it's true that it's better to be riding in a limousine than pedalling a bicycle when you're crying, but I wouldn't be you for the world, Xavier. You might have all this money and you might own the motel I love, but at least I know how to *love* people—at least I know how to make them feel wanted and valued.'

'That is enough!'

A cold hand squeezed his heart. *He was not like his grandmother*!

'From now on we are nothing more than colleagues. One more insult...'

The threat hung in the air between them. Her eyes told him what a piece of work she thought him.

He forced himself to continue. 'From now on you will address me with respect! Do I make myself clear?'

'Yes, *sir*.'

That *sir* stung. He drew himself up, though his stomach churned. 'Luis and I will be going to Sydney. You have one month to complete the refurbishment of Villa Lorenzo. If you think you can manage it.'

She tilted her chin. 'In my sleep!'

'I will return to inspect the motel, and then Luis and I will be returning to Spain. Is that clear?'

'Crystal.'

When she didn't move he raised an eyebrow. 'Is there anything else?'

Without another word Wynne turned on her heel and strode from the room, slamming the door behind her.

With a groan, Xavier sank into the nearest chair and dropped his head to his hands.

'From now on you will address me with respect! Do I make myself clear?'

The force of her anger had spots forming at the edges of Wynne's vision.

'We are nothing more than colleagues.'

Her hands clenched.

'Is there anything else?'

Nothing save the receipt spike she'd like to stick through his chest, or the paperweight she'd like to pelt at his head, or…

Halfway down the front staircase she slammed to a halt, all her bloodthirsty impulses coalescing into a perfect plan for revenge. Her heart pounded.

Noooo, she couldn't!

She closed her eyes, her anger corralling the pain until she could breathe again. She lifted her chin.

Oh, yes she could.

It would cost her the job she loved, but that would be a small price to pay.

She stalked the rest of the way down the staircase, resolution lending strength to her legs.

Tina glanced up, but her smile died on her lips. 'Whoa! Are you okay?'

'Get me Bradford and Sons on the phone… please.'

Without another word, Tina did so.

'Mr Bradford? It's Wynne Stephens. Listen, the brief for Villa Lorenzo has changed.' She explained the changes. 'Can you deliver?'

'Absolutely,' the builder assured her.

'Excellent. Can you have it done in a month?'

'Easily.'

'When can you start?'

'Monday?'

'Perfect.'

She dropped the phone.

'Oh, Wynne!' Tina fell down onto her stool. 'What have you done?'

She tossed her hair back over her shoulder. 'This is what he does—he incites people to retaliate. No wonder revenge dogs him wherever he goes.' A grim smile built through her. 'I'm going to enjoy every moment of the next month.'

She stalked off, doing her absolute best not to cry.

One month later…

Wynne strode into the foyer and turned on the spot, her eyes searching out every nook and cranny. She was aware of Tina's scrutiny from the check-in counter. Dusting off her hands, she turned to her second-in-command and made herself smile.

But if the truth be told her ability to smile—to

really smile—had deserted her...oh, about a month ago now. Tina's grimace told her she hadn't suddenly reacquired the ability.

Tina cleared her throat. 'Did Xavier give you an ETA?'

His name made her pulse leap, and she hated herself for it. She'd spent the last month fuelled by anger. She'd probably spend the next month crying. So be it.

'He said they'd be here at three-thirty p.m.'

After today she'd probably never see him again.

She tossed her head. You could lead a horse to water, but you couldn't make him drink. You could give a man your heart, but you couldn't force him to accept it.

But she *could* force him to confront the sterility of the world he'd shut himself away in.

She glanced around again, trying to harness her racing pulse. 'Everything looks shipshape.'

'Is that what you call it?' Tina muttered.

'I'd call it soulless.' Her heart hammered in her chest as a limousine glided down the driveway. 'Which is utterly perfect.'

No matter how much she tried, she couldn't make her pulse slow or prevent her heart from beating too hard as Luis and then Xavier emerged from the car. Her eyes locked with Xavier's for the briefest of moments through the glass doors, but he didn't smile, and his glance acknowledged...nothing.

'I am your employer. You will treat me with respect.'

She lifted her chin. *Game on.*

Luis burst into the foyer and ran straight for her, flinging his arms about her waist. 'We did so much in Sydney, Tía Wynne. I have lots to tell you. And...' he glanced around '...this place looks lots different.'

She knelt down and gave him a hug. She had no intention of punishing him for his father's sins. 'I can't wait to hear all your news. And, yes, while you were away we made some changes.' She held him at arm's length. 'I swear you've grown at least an inch in the last month.'

She rose, aware of Xavier's bulk just behind Luis. 'Good afternoon, Mr Ramos, I trust you had a pleasant journey?'

His eyes narrowed as he glanced around. For a moment she thought he meant to take her to task—for her formality, or perhaps for the new style of foyer—but he merely drew himself up and with a cold nod said, 'Perfect, thank you.'

'Tía Wynne! Where will I play?'

Luis stood in the doorway of the old drawing room, which was now a brand spanking new breakfast room. His crestfallen face speared into her heart.

'For the moment you can play in my back garden with Blake and Heath. They've been waiting for you to arrive.'

With a whoop, he disappeared.

She turned back to Xavier. 'I expect you'd like to retire to your room to freshen up after your journey.'

'Then you expect wrong. I have been looking forward to afternoon tea in the drawing room.'

She assumed her most innocent expression. 'I'm afraid we didn't organise one this time. Our last effort received such a lukewarm response that we thought it wouldn't be appreciated.'

She had, however, set up afternoon tea in her garden for the boys. She had no intention of telling *him* that, though. Her back garden belonged to *her*. The motel belonged to him. He was the one who had decided that *never the twain should meet*.

His face twisted as he turned a full circle. 'What have you done?'

'Refurbishment according to your brief.' His original brief—the one in which he'd wanted everything matching and uniform rather than the Spanish theme that she'd later talked him into. 'You'll see the colour scheme is an inoffensive blue-grey—nice and neutral. It should stand the test of time.'

He gestured to the skylight. 'This scheme of yours is sucking the very light out of the room.'

'Your scheme, not mine.' She sent him the fakest smile she could muster. '*Your* motel, *not* mine.'

He strode across to the doorway of the new morning room. Whatever he saw there made his spine rigid. When he turned back he had a face like thunder.

She didn't give him the opportunity to speak, but turned to Tina, who was watching all that was unfolding as if it were a car wreck she couldn't drag her gaze from.

'Tina, I believe the phone is ringing.'

Tina snapped to attention and Wynne moved behind the counter to check in the elderly couple who'd just arrived. It took a concerted effort to suppress her natural warmth and exuberance, but she managed it.

Xavier stormed across once they'd disappeared. 'What was *that*? It…it bordered on rudeness!'

'Nonsense. It was nothing of the sort. We have a new motto here at Villa Lorenzo. Efficiency is king—quiet efficiency…the quieter the better. We've come to understand that it's efficiency you value rather than hospitality. And nobody can accuse us of not doing our best to please.'

His jaw dropped.

She walked over to the breakfast room. 'What do you think? You said you wanted a breakfast room.'

His brows snapped down low over his eyes. 'There is nowhere for the guests to sit in comfort after dinner.'

'Villa Lorenzo doesn't serve dinner, so that seemed surplus to requirements.'

'Where will Luis play?'

'Your remit didn't include a children's play area. I assumed that was surplus to requirements as well.'

His face turned so dark she wondered if he'd fire

her on the spot. Oh, no, he couldn't do that. Not before she'd had a chance to show him the *pièce de resistance*—the cherry on top of the cake. Besides, she still had quite a lot she wanted to say to him. But she meant to say it in in private—not in front of a gawking Tina or any guests who might wander in.

She sent him one of the polite, distant smiles she'd been practising in the mirror for the last four weeks. 'Seeing as you're not ready to retire to your room, perhaps you'd like a tour of the motel?'

His lips pressed together, but he gestured for her to lead the way.

She took him through the ground-floor rooms first. They were carbon copies of each other—all of them clean, characterless, and mind-numbingly boring. He said nothing, but she could feel him growing tenser and tighter.

She led him up the back stairs. 'You'll notice that we dispensed with the wooden bannisters and balustrades. These stainless steel ones are far more serviceable.'

'And ugly.'

'They're also very well made. The best that money can buy.'

'You think *this* is what I want?'

He hadn't once asked her how she was, hadn't smiled at her…hadn't even said hello. She understood that she hadn't given him much opportunity to do so, but he was a grown man—he had the ability to act on his own initiative instead of acting merely in reaction to her and the schedule she set.

So she had no compunction in saying, 'My understanding of what you want is an environment that is cool and dispassionate, where efficiency rules, and where overfamiliarity and individuality are not encouraged. Naturally with quality furnishings and fittings in place. I believe Villa Lorenzo provides all those things in spades.'

'Where is the Captain?' he suddenly bellowed.

She turned to find him staring at the anonymous abstract print where the Captain's picture had once held pride of place. His outrage almost gave her cause for hope.

Almost, but not quite. She wasn't a total fantasist. 'Probably in a skip somewhere.'

He gaped at her. 'You tossed him out with the garbage?'

Of course she hadn't—he was in her living room—but Xavier didn't need to know that. 'Correct me if I'm wrong, but I seem to recall you saying the picture was clichéd. I took that to mean that there was no room in your universe for the Captain.'

His mouth snapped shut. His lips pressed into a hard, thin line. Those lips had once taken her to heaven. And then they'd uttered such ugly, harsh words they'd dropped her into the depths of hell.

'Wynne?'

She'd been staring! She shook herself. 'Yes…sir?'

He ground his jaw so hard that if he wasn't

careful he'd snap a tooth. 'The motel is hideous! I hate it.'

'That's surprising.'

'You've made it look sterile, anonymous...*cold*.'

'Yes, but that's the other side of the coin—if you want efficiency and reserve then...' she gestured around '...this is what you get.'

'What happened to the Spanish theme?'

'Oh, but that was Aggie's dream...and we both know you didn't come here to bring *her* dreams to life—quite the opposite, in fact.'

She came to a halt outside the Windsor Suite, now renamed the Lorenzo Suite. She wanted to bring this awful interview to an end. She unlocked the door and led the way, trying to suppress a shudder at the utter starkness of the room.

Xavier halted in the doorway. 'It looks like a prison cell.'

'That's the effect I was aiming for.'

A pulse at his jaw pounded. 'Have you enjoyed your revenge?'

She nodded, but not in agreement. 'It started out as revenge, Xavier, that's true enough.'

He blinked, but whether at the fact she'd called him by his name or at her candour she had no way of knowing.

She moved further into the room, past the bed and into the living area. 'Close the door, Xavier.'

He made no move to step inside the room. 'Aren't you afraid that I'll throttle you?'

She turned. 'You won't lay a finger on me.'

He raised one of those lethally dangerous eyebrows.

She merely sent him one of her custom-designed, teeth-achingly pleasant smiles in response. 'You've already broken my heart, and I believe that knowledge has you shaking in your highly polished leather lace-ups. I hold no fears for my neck.'

With a savage movement he moved into the room and let the door shut behind him. It did nothing so crass as to slam—she'd made sure that everything in the motel was as controlled and repressed as he was.

Which was why she had to leave.

She could never fit into this world. She didn't want to.

She pointed. 'Note the opposing portraits.'

She'd encased Aggie and Lorenzo's portraits in glass cases and they now faced each other from opposite walls.

Xavier's eyes flashed dark fire. 'No doubt you mean to explain the stripes you've had painted on them?'

'They're prison bars, of course. But—just so you know—it's my own handiwork.' She didn't want anyone else blamed for it. 'The bars aren't painted on the portraits themselves, just on the glass. It appears that I'm not destructive enough to actually deface a portrait.'

'And your point is…?'

He looked as if he might actually have ice running through his veins, and she suddenly felt exhausted. 'Oh, I have more than one point to make, but now that we come to it I find I've lost my appetite for it.' She gave a short laugh. 'I suppose it's because I know in my heart that it's only worthwhile making a point if it's a catalyst for change. And I have no such hope here.'

She huffed out a breath.

'Still, for what it's worth, you have to realise by now that the motel is a reflection of you and your world, how you choose to live—'

'How *you* view my world,' he shot at her. '*Your* interpretation.'

That snapped some fire back into her blood. 'You live your life along these same sterile lines, and I have no intention of wasting my warmth and my hospitality where they're not valued!'

He paled at her words.

'You wanted Villa Lorenzo to be a homage to your grandfather.' She pointed at Lorenzo's portrait. 'He was a man who ran away rather than risking all for love. What did that earn him? From what I can tell, nothing but regrets. I might've been the one to draw bars on the glass, but he's the one who put himself behind them. He's the one who sentenced himself to living a half-life.'

Xavier clenched his hands so hard he started to shake. 'You didn't know him.'

'And you living like this…in all your isolated glory! *This* is how you want to honour his memory? Can't you see what a mockery you're making of the man who went adventuring with you in the old town, who played with you and loved you? Do you think he'd be happy at this life you've carved out for yourself? Do you think he'd be happy to see you running away from love, just like he did?'

'Don't you—'

'Is *that* the legacy you want to leave for Luis?' The words left her at a bellow.

Xavier's face contorted and he stabbed a finger at her. 'You're—'

'Fired?'

They stared at each other, breathing hard.

'You'll find my letter of resignation on your desk there.' She pointed.

And then she turned to the portrait opposite Lorenzo's and did what she could to get her breathing back under control.

'I don't know why Aggie didn't go after him, but I have no intention of making the same mistake she did.'

She strode over to Xavier, seized him by his pristine silk tie and slammed her lips to his. She didn't kiss him like a good girl. She didn't kiss him like a wild woman. But she did kiss him with her whole heart.

She released him and took a step back before his

arms could slip about her waist. 'I love you, Xavier. If you ever find your courage, look me up.'

She left then, and didn't look back.

CHAPTER TWELVE

XAVIER WASN'T SURE how long he stood there after Wynne had gone, but once the roaring in his ears and the rush of his blood had died down he grew aware once again of the oppressive silence, the utter sterility of the room. His heart kicked in savage protest as he turned on the spot.

His life looked *nothing* like this! He had colour in his life—he had love and…and happiness. He had success. And he had Luis.

His mouth dried. *When was the last time you had fun?*

He had fun playing with Luis—teaching him to kick a ball, taking him to the beach, reading him a bedtime story.

When was the last time you had fun that didn't depend on Luis?

He raked both hands back through his hair. *The week he and Wynne had been lovers.* He wasn't referring to the lovemaking—as spectacular as it had been. While it was hard to banish the heat of her kisses from his mind, it was her laughter he found himself missing the most.

She said that she loved you.

He pushed that thought from his mind. The last time he'd had fun before Wynne…?

He couldn't remember.

And he couldn't tolerate this room another moment!

He slammed out of it and made his way down to the foyer. Tina glanced up at him, but she didn't speak.

'Wynne?' he croaked.

She swallowed. 'Gone.'

Already the motel felt empty without her, and Tina looked ready to cry. He had no comfort to offer her. 'The motel, the changes…they're awful.'

She moistened her lips. 'I don't know what you did to her, Xavier. I've never seen her like that before. But…' She glanced around. 'Did you deserve this?'

She told you she loved you!

His shoulders suddenly sagged. 'Yes.'

'Well, then—' she folded her arms '—how do you propose to make things right again?'

He couldn't make things right for Wynne. For the sake of his heart he had to stay away from her. He had to—

Coward.

He braced his arms against the counter. She'd told him she loved him—fearlessly—and yet there'd been no expectation in her face that he'd return the sentiment. There had been pain there, yes, but not defeat.

How could that be? Why wasn't she afraid of being vanquished and diminished in the same way

Lorenzo had been afraid? The way Xavier himself was afraid?

Do not make the same mistakes I made.

'Xavier?'

He snapped to attention at the worry in Tina's voice. 'I cannot stay in the Lorenzo Suite. Have you seen it?'

She shook her head.

'Luis and I will stay in the…what did she rename the Westminster Suite?'

'The Family Suite.'

She said it with a curl of her lip as she handed him the key. He didn't blame her. *The Family Suite* sounded utterly devoid of personality.

'How have the regular guests taken the changes?'

'They've been too busy keeping their heads down below the parapet.'

Por Dios! Had he turned the welcoming Wynne into a raging she-devil?

'And the staff?' *Joder!* 'Please tell me that Libby and April and…and everyone else are still working here?'

'Yes, but they're not adapting so well to this new regime of efficiency over hospitality. They'll get there, but please be patient with them. They—'

'*No!*' *Dios.* Tina thought this was what he *wanted*? 'We go back to the old way of doing things! Hospitality first. There must be carnations for Ms What's-her-Name's room. And we need to find the

Captain, and…and…and all of this dreary grey—it must go!'

The tension in Tina's shoulders melted. 'Thank you, God!'

He didn't know if it was a prayer or an utterance of thanksgiving. 'Can you make an appointment for the builders to come and see me as soon as it can be arranged?'

'I…uh…already took the liberty of arranging that. They'll be here at nine o'clock in the morning.'

'Perfect.' He went to turn away, but at the last moment swung back. 'She is not coming back, is she?'

Tina's eyes welled. 'No.'

It felt as if the ground beneath his feet was dropping away. She had said that she loved him and he had said nothing. He had done *nothing*.

Luis came racing into the foyer to fling his arms around Xavier's waist. 'I made a six!' With a whoop he raced back out again.

Without Wynne's insight and her generosity—her willingness to involve herself in the lives of others—it would have taken him far longer to bridge the gulf that had opened between him and his son. It occurred to him then that on his own he might never have managed it.

On his own…

He lurched towards the stairs. He wasn't on his own any more. Wynne had welcomed him into her eccentric makeshift family, and even now they surrounded him, supported him. But where was *she*?

She'd gone. She'd given him *everything* and then she'd left. He'd driven her out.

He halted on the stairs, his every muscle freezing. *'Dios!'* His hand clenched around the cold stainless steel railing. He was such a fool. She'd offered him her heart—something more precious than all his wealth—and he'd spurned her because…because he was afraid of being made a fool of, afraid of being shackled into a cold and loveless marriage?

Do not make the same mistakes I made.

Lorenzo hadn't meant for Xavier to run away from love. He'd meant that Xavier should embrace it! His mouth dried as he realised the full extent of his foolishness.

He was afraid of shadows! Wynne didn't possess a cold bone in her body. Her love had never come with conditions—unlike his grandmother, unlike Camilla.

He swung back to Tina. 'I know how to make it right!'

She raised her hands heavenwards. 'Hallelujah!'

He just had to give back all he had taken from her.

'She still might not forgive me.' But it was a risk he had to take.

It was time to dispense with the selfishness of his solitude and do what Wynne did—fight to make the world a better place. He owed it to Wynne. He owed it to Luis. He owed it to Lorenzo.

Most of all, he owed it to himself.

* * *

The builders started work immediately. Xavier paid top dollar to hire more labourers. They thought he was crazy, but he didn't care. All he wanted to do was put things right.

He wanted to win Wynne's heart too. But that decision would ultimately rest with her. In the meantime he threw himself into overseeing the renovations and helping to run the motel.

'Xavier!'

He pulled up short when Mrs Montgomery wheeled her suitcase out of her room.

He held the door open for her. 'Are you leaving us today?'

'I'm afraid so, but before I go I wanted to thank you. I followed your advice to the letter and the general manager has agreed to give me a raise.'

'That is most excellent news!' He took her suitcase and walked her to the foyer. 'I'm glad the man saw sense. Now I will leave you in Tina's capable hands while I take your case to your car…and we will see you in a fortnight's time, yes?'

Xavier pulled to a halt. He could hear crying.

The housekeeping trolley stood pressed against the wall nearby. He glanced through the open door of the nearest room to find Libby sitting on the stripped bed, the sheets bundled up in her arms and her face pressed into them as her shoulders shook.

He glanced up and down the corridor, but April

was nowhere in sight. He pressed a fist to his mouth and stared at the sobbing girl. He couldn't just leave her. Wynne wouldn't leave her.

Gingerly he entered and sat on the bed to pat the sobbing girl's back. 'Why are you crying, Libby? Do you feel sick?'

She shook her head. 'I miss Miss Wynne.' She started to sob harder. 'She was my friend.'

Regardless of the changes he was in the process of overseeing—and they were a definite improvement, reflected in an increase in both guest satisfaction and staff morale—the place wasn't the same without Wynne. An ache opened up inside him. She'd offered him everything. He couldn't believe that he hadn't had the wit to seize it in both hands and hold it close. *What an idiot!*

'I miss her too.'

Libby lifted her head. 'You do?'

More than anyone could possibly know.

'Maybe we can talk her into visiting some time soon—maybe for afternoon tea. That'd be nice, wouldn't it?'

She nodded.

A movement in the doorway alerted him to April's presence.

'Are you ladies busy this evening? We could have a staff pizza and pavlova night.' Pavlova had become Luis's newest favourite thing. 'Everyone has been working so hard it'd be nice to relax for a bit, yes?'

Both women agreed with flattering enthusiasm.

'April, can you spare Libby for the next half an hour?'

'Yes, sir.'

'Xavier,' he corrected gently, for what must have been the thirtieth time in the past week. 'Libby, would you like to go downstairs and help Luis with his jigsaw puzzle? He would welcome the company.'

With a big grin she raced off.

'Don't run!' both he and April hollered after her.

The older woman turned to him. 'You're good with her.'

'She is missing Wynne. It is only to be expected.'

Shrewd eyes met his. 'Seems we're all missing her, Xavier.'

Maybe he wasn't doing as good a job at hiding his heart as he'd thought.

He strode from the room, hoping he was doing enough to win Wynne's heart. If he wasn't...

A stone lodged in his chest. If he wasn't he had no one to blame but himself. He squared his shoulders. It would tear at his soul—he couldn't deny it—but he'd refuse to let it force him back into the shell of isolation that had almost consumed him. He'd learned his lesson. Life was for living, and that was exactly what he meant to do—*live*.

Wynne had to leave the Gold Coast following her resignation—just for a week. She couldn't stand staying in her little cottage knowing that Xavier was so close…and that despite laying her heart on the line it had had such little impact on him.

She tossed her head. She didn't regret saying what she had. She could only surmise what had happened between Aggie and Lorenzo all those years ago but, while they'd obviously loved each other, they'd not had their happy-ever-after. Wynne had no intention of repeating whatever mistakes they might have made. She refused to be a victim of the pride and fear she suspected had held them back. She didn't want to die wondering, *What if I'd spoken up…?*

She snorted. 'Well, you don't have to worry about that any more.' She could now die safe in the knowledge that it hadn't made a jot of difference. She lifted her arms and let them drop, her lips twisting. 'Oh, and that knowledge is *such* a comfort!'

The first thing she did when she returned to Surfer's Paradise was to visit Aggie—even before she returned home. It had killed her to leave her grandmother for the week, but she'd phoned every day. Aggie had no idea who Wynne was, but she happily accepted a bar of chocolate and played a cheerful hand of Old Maid with her.

Old Maid seemed particularly appropriate. 'Like grandmother like granddaughter.'

'What was that, dear?'

'Nothing, Nanna, just muttering to myself.'

Not long after she took her leave and finally returned home. She did a double take at all the activity next door.

'Don't look!' she ordered herself. It was no concern of hers.

Though how could she *not* look? It appeared that Xavier had hired every tradesman in the Gold Coast to come and work on Villa Lorenzo.

What did you expect? He would never settle for that ghastly décor she'd thrust on him. It was hardly surprising that he'd set to work on it ASAP.

She strode through her front door and shut it tight, her heart hammering in her chest. What was surprising was that Xavier was still here. He should have left for Spain days ago.

How do you know he's there? You didn't see him.

She didn't need to see him. Only Xavier could create such a sense of purpose in those around him. She wanted to ring Tina for the gossip, but she forced herself not to. Her best course of action was to try and forget Xavier completely.

Ha! Good luck with that.

Two days later Wynne received a gilded invitation to attend the grand opening of the new motel that had once been called Aggie's Retreat, and then briefly named Villa Lorenzo. Briefly? Had Xavier decided to call it something else instead? The date for the grand opening was in a fortnight's time.

Come and see the unveiling of the motel's new name.

With a snort, she tossed the envelope into the bin. 'He should call it the Heartbreak Hotel.'

Unable to dwell on that thought with any equanimity, she went to search her cupboards for chocolate.

'What do you mean, you're not coming?'

'Look, Tina, it's not a difficult concept to grasp.'

Wynne rested the phone against her shoulder as she poured hot water into a mug and jiggled a teabag in it. She'd given up coffee. The high levels of caffeine she'd been consuming recently were making it impossible for her to sleep at night.

'But we all so want you to come!'

'Of course you do—you're my friends and you care about me. And I know you're worried about me, but I'm fine. I promise.'

'Then come to the opening and prove it.'

'Is *he* going to be there?'

'Xavier? Yes, of course.'

'Then, no.'

'Come for the rest of us.'

She bit her lip and swallowed. 'This is going to sound harsh, so I apologise in advance, but I'm tired of putting everyone else's needs and wants before my own. I don't want to see him. I don't want to be there. I won't be coming. Why don't we catch up for dinner one night next week?'

And then, like a coward—*like Xavier*—she hung up before Tina could argue with her further.

Unable to dwell on that thought with any equanimity, she reached into the back of the pantry and pulled out half a packet of chocolate melts—the last chocolate she had in the house.

She made a note to stock up on chocolate before Saturday—the night of the opening. She had a feeling she'd need a whole family block to get her through that night.

Saturday night.

She should have gone out!

Wynne watched the car park next door fill up and kicked herself for not having organised to go to the movies or…or just down to the tavern on the corner for a quiet meal and maybe a game of pool.

Heck! Even takeaway fish and chips on the beach would be better than sitting here, aware that her friends were all next door, no doubt enjoying champagne and artistic little canapés.

No, not fish and chips on the beach. That reminded her too much of Luis…and Xavier. Pain pierced her chest, so sharp it made her buckle at the waist. Breathing hard, she lowered herself to the sofa, determined not to cry, but…

Would she ever stop wanting him?

Laughter from next door floated in through her open living room window. She went to close it—to shut it out—but stopped short. Her breath suddenly came in short, sharp gasps.

She sat. What was she doing, shutting laughter out of her life? How would *that* help her get over a broken heart? She'd been disappointed in love. So what? Was she now going to become a bitter recluse?

She shot to her feet. She'd sold Xavier her motel, but she hadn't sold her soul!

Storming into her bedroom, she pulled on her best dress, donned her highest heels, and slicked on her reddest lipstick. She'd sashay into Aggie's Retreat… Villa Lorenzo…or whatever the heck it was called these days, with so much style and aplomb and…and grace that it would make Xavier Ramos eat his heart out.

Wynne walked around to the front of the motel rather than take the shortcut through the gate in her side fence. There was a new sign—currently covered—that would add its neon glow to all the others that lined this Surfers Paradise strip.

At the door she was met by a tuxedo-clad doorman. 'Do you have your invitation, ma'am?'

She had a vision of her invitation sitting among chocolate wrappers and vegetable peelings. 'I'm afraid not.'

'Then I'm sorry, but—'

'My name is Wynne Stephens.' She nodded to the clipboard he held. 'I think you'll find my name there.'

He snapped to attention. 'At the very top!'

She had to grin in spite of herself. 'You have to hand it to Xavier—he has class.'

He gestured to a waiter and handed her a glass of champagne. 'Enjoy your evening, Ms Stephens.'

She took three steps into the crowded foyer before coming to a dead stop. *Dear God!* Xavier had...

For a moment her vision blurred. Xavier had returned Aggie's Retreat to its full former Victorian manor glory. Except the motel had *never* looked this good. The brand-new Axminster carpet, embellished with rich swirls of gold, fawn and pale blue, added an elegance that she'd only ever dreamed about. The chandelier gracing the ceiling looked original, while the gleaming wood of the check-in counter, the staircase and the drawing room doors looked like real oak rather than stained pine fakes. It all looked...

It looked like her dream! Her grandmother had dreamed of Spain, but Wynne had dreamed of this.

Had Xavier seen the same potential she had?

All the hairs on her arms lifted. All she needed to do was turn her head and she would find him on the stairs. She was certain of it.

Play it cool.

She took a further two steps into the space full of sparkling light and lively chatter, took a sip of her champagne, and then let her glance idly turn towards the gorgeous gleaming staircase.

They stared at each other for several heart-stopping beats, and the hunger that flared momentarily in his eyes made her tremble. One look! Yet it was enough to fire her blood with heat and turn her knees to water. She wanted to run to him and tell him she loved what he'd done with the motel. Instead she raised her glass, as if in toast, and then moved towards the drawing room. He made no move towards her. She didn't know whether to be disappointed or relieved.

'Miss Wynne!'

In no time at all Wynne found herself surrounded by her old staff as well as long-standing guests of the motel and it felt like being home.

Except she was constantly aware of Xavier, moving among the guests in the background. He kept his distance which, given the heat in his gaze whenever their eyes locked, was just as well. She made a mental note to leave early. The man could tempt her to anything, but the one thing she *didn't* want to do was wake up beside him in the morning and have to say goodbye all over again.

So she ate glorious little canapés and sipped her French bubbly sparingly and badgered Tina to give her a tour of the motel's guest rooms.

'Tomorrow,' Tina promised. 'They're all booked out tonight.'

All of them? She traced a finger around the rim of her champagne flute. 'Do you know what the motel's new name is?'

Tina's sudden grin had curiosity shifting through her.

'Give,' she ordered. 'What is it?'

'Looks like you're about to find out.'

Tina nodded behind her and Wynne glanced around to find Xavier calling for everyone to move into the foyer. He stood behind the check-in counter while the guests filled the foyer, the staircase and the first floor landing. He'd invited some of the Gold Coast's leading businesspeople, the odd celebrity, and the press. Cameras flashed all around them.

Wynne tried to make her way to the back of the crowd, but Tina pulled her to one side of the drawing room doors, beside a potted palm that gave her some measure of cover at least.

'I want to thank all of you for joining me this evening to celebrate the opening of this most excellent of motels. I never knew what a treasure I would find when I first came here, and I think you will all agree that—now, let me see if I can get this right… I have been getting an education in the Australian vernacular—*it scrubs up all right, mate.*'

Laughter and applause greeted him. Wynne straightened. Xavier seemed so relaxed and at ease. She'd never seen him that relaxed.

'Working on this motel has been a life-changing experience for me. Getting to know the staff here, and the regular guests, has made me understand that there are things in this world more important than shareholder profits and owning a company jet.'

She swallowed. She'd be a fool to trust his words. He was just playing to the audience.

'Do you think he owns his own jet?' she whispered to Tina.

Tina shushed her.

'I owe an enormous debt of gratitude to one woman in particular. She made me pull my head out of the sand and smell the roses.'

'Mixed metaphor,' she whispered.

Tina dug her in the ribs. 'Be quiet!'

'She's the woman who created a culture of warmth and hospitality here that is truly unique.'

Oh! She pressed a hand to her chest. He was going to honour Aggie!

'And in honour of that woman I now want to unveil the motel's new name.'

He reached up and she suddenly noticed that a covered portrait hung where Aggie's portrait had always hung.

'I give you…the Welcoming Wynne.'

He pulled the cord to unveil a portrait of…*her!*

A cheer went up and the crowd applauded. Wynne was barely aware of it as she stared at the picture of herself—complete with wide smile and dancing eyes.

'Please—the night is yet young.'

Xavier's voice cut through her stupor.

'There is more food to be eaten, more wine to be drunk, and there will be dancing in the drawing room shortly.

And then he was making a beeline straight for her!

'Good God, Tina, why didn't you—?' She turned, but Tina was nowhere to be seen.

'Hello, Wynne.'

She nodded and swallowed. 'Xavier.'

He gestured around. 'What do you think? Do you like it?'

'I love it.' She glanced at the check-in desk, the potted palm, the people on the stairs…anywhere but at him. 'You've made it look as wonderful as I always dreamed it could. How…?'

How could he have seen inside her head?

'I found a drawer full of your magazine cuttings. They made me see your vision for the motel.'

Her heart jammed in her throat.

'I wanted to pay tribute…to you. They showed me the perfect way I could achieve that.'

'Why?' The question croaked out of her. 'Why would you want to do something like that? Guilt?'

'Not guilt, Wynne.' He shook his head. 'For love. In an attempt to win your heart.'

The room swayed. She couldn't have heard him right. But Xavier went right on talking.

'I needed something more than an apology—something bigger—to show you that I've realised you were right…I've been hiding from love when I should've been embracing it.'

They were standing in the middle of a crowded room and he…he was talking about *love*? This couldn't be real. It had to be a dream.

'Pinch me!' she ordered.

He merely smiled. 'I needed a grand gesture like this to…'

Her breath stuttered in her chest. 'To?'

'To make amends.'

How…*dreary.*

'And to tell you that I love you.'

Cameras flashed, laughter and chatter sounded all around and threatened to overwhelm his simple statement. She set her champagne flute onto a passing waiter's tray before planting her hands on her hips.

'Excuse me, but I thought you just said…'

He grinned, and she found it utterly infuriating.

Lifting her chin, she glared at him. 'Are you still staying in the Windsor Suite?'

'I am.'

Without another word, she seized his hand, pulled him through the crowd and up the staircase, and then along the hushed corridor to the very last door on the right. Without a word, he unlocked the door. She pushed through it first, stomped into the middle of the room—and then bit back a groan. A four-poster bed, complete with a gorgeous floral comforter, and real antique rosewood furniture greeted her stunned gaze. It was divine!

Xavier leaned against the wall, smiling at her shock. He raised one of those eyebrows. 'Now that you have me here, what are you going to do with me?'

'Beat you up.' But the threat came out huskily…
and was no threat at all.

He pushed away from the wall, his smile fading as he came to stand in front of her. 'I love you,
Wynne. You've shown me what a gift life can be if
I let friendship and love into my heart rather than
keeping it at arm's length. I never knew. I didn't
realise that love could make so much difference.'

Because apart from Luis, no one other than
Lorenzo had ever loved him properly—not the way
he deserved to be loved.

'I understand I might have ruined things between
us for good. I understand if you do not want to give
me another chance to prove I am worthy of you.'

She opened her mouth, but he pressed a finger
to her lips.

'But I want you to know, even if that is the case,
that I have learned my lesson. I will not be shutting
myself off from life again.'

Her heart thumped against her ribcage. 'You really mean that?'

He nodded.

'That's why I came tonight,' she whispered. 'I
realised that cutting myself off from my friends
wouldn't help me get over a broken heart.'

'It is the same reason I have had the deeds of the
motel transferred into your name.'

She took a step back. 'I sold you the motel fair
and square, Xavier. It's yours.'

He shook his head. 'The heart of this motel is *you*,

Wynne.' He seized an envelope from a nearby table and pressed it into her hands. 'The motel is yours. It always was.'

Tears clogged her throat.

'You have given me far more than bricks and mortar ever could. And I am hoping you will let me share in that life with you.'

To her amazement he went down on one knee and opened a tiny box to reveal a ring—a sparkling diamond ring.

'Wynne Stephens, I love you. I want to spend the rest of my life proving just how much. Will you do me the very great honour of becoming my wife?'

She stopped trying to play it cool then. She flung her arms around his neck. 'Yes!'

With a whoop, he stood and swung her around. Then very slowly he let her body slide down the full length of his before cupping her face and kissing her.

It was a long time before he lifted his head again, and when he did they were both breathing hard. In a smooth movement he lifted her off her feet and strode across the room to the leather chesterfield sofa, where he settled her on his lap.

He loved her. He really loved her. She could barely take it in.

He brushed the hair from her face. 'I've thought about it carefully. I know you cannot leave Aggie. So Luis and I will live here with you.'

She straightened, still tingling from their kiss.

'But what about your work?' He had a huge corporation to run.

He dismissed that with a single wave of his hand. 'I am tired of work. I will hire managers. I want to work here with you.'

Really? 'Have you spoken to Luis? How will he feel about that?'

'I forgot! Here.' He pulled an envelope from his jacket pocket. 'It is from Luis.'

It was a handmade card that read, *Please marry Papà*. It had a picture of the three of them making a sandcastle on the beach.

She pressed the card to her chest, blinking hard. 'Oh!'

'Maybe later on we can spend six months of the year here and the other six months in Spain. I know that there are issues, and problems to be faced, but Camilla is Luis's mother. I need to do what I can to repair and promote her relationship with Luis. I want to do that.'

She pressed her hand to his chest, to the spot over his heart—such a big, warm heart. 'I think that's the right thing to do too.'

'It might not work.'

'But you have to try. And if it doesn't work then Luis will always have you…and me. I love him too, Xavier. I promise to always put his needs first.'

His fingers traced a path along her jawline and down her throat to skim the neckline of her dress.

Her breath hitched and her blood flooded with heat. She wanted to fall into him, but first…

'I love you, Xavier.'

His gaze darkened.

'And now that you have me, neither you nor Luis are ever going to be alone again.'

He pressed a kiss to the corner of her mouth.

'So that means you'll have me and Luis…and all the other children that are bound to come along.'

He stilled. 'You want children?'

She ran her hand over his chest, relishing the solid male feel of him. 'I want oodles of children.'

'Oodles? This is how many?'

'At least four.'

His grin, when it came, was full of wonder.

She tossed her head. 'So, you see, that means you'll have me and Luis…and Samantha.'

'Samantha?'

'It's my favourite girl's name. Do you like it? Then there'll be…'

'Carlos?' he offered.

'And Little Aggie and Lorenzo Junior,' she finished.

He started to laugh. 'And Libby and April, and Tina, Blake and Heath, and…'

'And everyone else,' she agreed, laughing with him.

He stared down at her with so much love in his eyes it stole her breath.

She pulled his head down to hers. 'The Welcoming Wynne, huh? Let's see if I can't give you a welcome that you'll never forget.'

The low rumble of his laughter and the warmth of his lips on hers sealed the silent promise they made to each other—to live and to love. Whatever else life might hold, they could hold fast to that, and to each other. Forever.

* * * * *

#4567 CONVENIENTLY WED TO THE GREEK
by Kandy Shepherd
Greek tycoon Alex Mikhalis will do whatever it takes to get even with the blogger who nearly destroyed his reputation—only guarded Adele Hudson isn't exactly like he remembers. And when Alex discovers she's pregnant, he soon suggests a very intimate solution: becoming his convenient wife!

#4568 HIS SHY CINDERELLA
by Kate Hardy
When racing driver Brandon Stone wants to buy her company, his shy business rival Angel McKenzie has no intention of selling! But Brandon ignites feelings in Angel she never knew existed. He's the last person she should *ever* date, but her heart is telling her to break the rules...

#4569 FALLING FOR THE REBEL PRINCESS
by Ellie Darkins
For successful music executive Charlie, AKA Princess Caroline of Afland, and rock star Joe Kavanagh, one night in Vegas changes everything... Their marriage is a PR dream come true for Joe, but as their initial attraction turns into something much deeper, can he convince Charlie that they were made for one other?

#4570 CLAIMED BY THE WEALTHY MAGNATE
The Derwent Family
by Nina Milne
One evening with wealthy lawyer Daniel Harrington makes Lady Kaitlin Derwent crave freedom from her tragic past... Daniel's never believed in love, but Kaitlin opens up new possibilities. Soon he's determined to show her that by being true to yourself you can find happiness—even in the most unexpected of places!

CONVENIENTLY WED TO THE GREEK
by **Kandy Shepherd**

*When Greek tycoon Alex Mikhalis discovers
Adele Hudson is pregnant, he abandons his plans
to get even and suggests a very intimate solution:
becoming his convenient wife!*

Read on for a sneak preview:

"What?" The word exploded from her. "You can't possibly be serious."

Alex looked down into her face. Even in the slanted light from the taverna she could see the intensity in his black eyes. "I'm very serious. I think we should get married."

Dell had never known what it felt to have her head spin. She felt it now. Alex had to take hold of her elbow to steady her. "I can't believe I'm hearing this," she said. "You said you'd never get married. I'm not pregnant to you. In fact you see my pregnancy as a barrier to kissing me, let alone marrying me. Have you been drinking too much ouzo?"

"Not a drop," he said. "It's my father's dying wish that I get married. He's been a good father. I haven't been a good son. Fulfilling that wish is important to me. If I have to get married, it makes sense that I marry you."

"It doesn't make a scrap of sense to me," she said. "You don't get married to someone to please someone else, even if it is your father."

Alex frowned. "You've misunderstood me. I'm not talking about a real marriage."

This was getting more and more surreal. "Not a real marriage? You mean a marriage of convenience?"

"Yes. Like people do to be able to get residence in a country. In this case it would be marriage to make my father happy. He wants the peace of mind of seeing me settled."

"You feel you owe your father?"

"I owe him so much it could never be calculated or repaid. This isn't about owing my father, it's about loving him. I love my father, Dell."

But you'll never love me, she cried in her heart. How could he talk about marrying someone—anyone— without a word about love?